# ROUGH NIGHT

SCREAMING DEMONS MC
BOOK EIGHT

SUMMER COOPER
SIENNA CHANCE

LOVY BOOKS

Lovy Books Ltd
20-22 Wenlock Road
London N1 7GU

Cover by SC Creative

1

---

*he heat caused sweat to cover his body, dripping from his clothes and skin. He felt disgusting and dirty. He could hear the drips of sweat fall into the well water beneath him. He had passed out, only waking when he heard a rattling from above him, it could be anything. A rat, a person, nothing. He didn't get his hopes up as he quietly hung, losing any hope of getting out. He knew he was most likely going to die, and he had accepted it. Probably no one had even noticed his disappearance. The blackness took him once again as he lost control of consciousness. The water below him started to swirl as if a plug had been pulled and he felt like he was about to be sucked up and spat out into nothing. His body shook with fear as he tried once more to find an escape, but there was nothing there that could help him, no one to save him. He watched as the water reached his waist, getting higher up his body as it covered his torso, then his shoulders and soon his mouth. He tried to hold onto the air he had left in his lungs, fighting against the burning sensation in his chest. He didn't know how much longer he could hold on for. His body started to rock as his lungs started to give in. It didn't take long before he was completely covered in darkness.*

*"It's okay, Sage, I'm here. I'm here," a voice called to him. He couldn't see the person's face, but he let go, trusting the voice. He gave up, he stopped fighting, and his body relaxed, he felt safe as warmth surrounded him. He didn't have to worry anymore, he was home, he was alive.*

Sage woke up in shock in the hospital the next day, alone. It took a bit of time for him to become fully aware of his surroundings as he almost started to panic, thinking he was still in the well, forgetting that he had been rescued by Mia and the Screaming Demons. He still couldn't believe that Mia had found him, the fact that she even searched for him shocked him. He knew he didn't deserve it after the way he had acted days before his disappearance, but nevertheless, he was grateful. He was in a bed, not his own bed yet but it was still better than hanging halfway down a dirty and dark well.

He knew he would be haunted with dreams of the well for a while. Not only had it been extremely dark down there but his mind had also gone to a dark place, a place darker than it had ever gone before. He knew he would have to work on getting his mind back to normal. It would just take some time to get over it all. He couldn't tell anyone about it though as he didn't want to seem weak. He was supposed to be an army man, after all. He'd been through tough situations before. He had managed to deal with it then and he'd manage to deal with it now.

His body ached and screamed at him with every movement he attempted to make. Even as he breathed his body cried in agony. He wondered if he had any broken bones, especially his knees after they had whacked them in order to take him. He couldn't imagine never being able to walk again. He tested his body, moving his feet and then slowly bending his knees, pleased and relieved when he felt them move beneath him. He was in pain, but he could move, and he was grateful for that.

He remembered Mia being there with him the night before, her body pressed against his in the small hospital bed. He could smell her perfume on the pillow, so he knew that he hadn't been dreaming, but she had clearly left before he woke up.

A part of him wished she was still there so he wouldn't be alone but he knew the world didn't stop turning just because he was in the hospital. She probably had the responsibility of cleaning up the rest of the mess he had caused and besides, he also knew he would need time alone. He hoped he hadn't screamed in his sleep which could've scared her away. He couldn't remember if he had had any dreams when he passed out but that didn't mean he didn't have one of his nightmares, especially after all the trauma he had just been through. He knew being in the well would now make his nightmares even worse. He had been closer to death and fully aware of it at the same time. He knew he might not be the same as he was three days ago. He didn't want to admit it but when he had had those moments down in the well, he wasn't always sure if they were real or not. He had become a little delusional and a part of him thought maybe he was imagining being in hospital. He had to grip onto the bed just to make sure it was real. He sighed with relief.

He tried to sit up but his body wouldn't allow it so he flopped back onto his back in defeat. He hated feeling so helpless. He was free of the well but he still felt trapped. His body weakened from the past couple of days, he might as well still be in the well. Don't think like that, he told himself. He had to be grateful that he was alive. He knew he had a lot of living still to do now that he had been so close to death once again.

He knew it would take a while for his body to fully recover after the two days in the well, which was confirmed when he was pulled out, but he had hoped his body wouldn't be in as much pain as it was. He wasn't sure if he'd have to stay in the hospital for a few more days but just the thought of it made him sad. He hated hospitals. He would have to work out even harder to get his muscles back. He took note of just how small he looked under the covers. To anyone else who knew him, they'd probably not notice much but he knew he had lost a good amount of weight and muscle.

"How are you feeling, Sage?" a voice said from the doorway. He wasn't sure how long the person had been standing there, hopefully not long enough to have seen him struggle with sitting up. He didn't want to look weak in front of people. He turned to look in the direction of the voice and was glad to see it was just a nurse. He wasn't ready to see Mia yet. She was a pretty nurse, almost middle-aged with a gentle smile, warm and trusting. Her name badge read Annabelle. She had a cute blonde bob haircut that just touched her shoulders which seemed to fit with her name. He smiled in return as she made her way into the room, checking his readings.

He remembered how Mia had held him after he had gotten out of the well and he wasn't sure how he would act around her when he saw her. He still needed some time to process everything so he was relieved she hadn't been the one at the door.

"My body is extremely sore but I'm just grateful to be here and alive," he replied. He knew if he hadn't been found he probably would've died down there. He could live with a few aches and pains for a while, but he wasn't at all ready for death. Of course, a part of him had wished for it when everything felt helpless but now that he was out and on the road to recovery he was glad he hadn't died. There was still so much he wanted to do.

He promised himself while he was down there that he would try harder at life if he survived and he intended to keep that promise. He remembered how he had thought about his team and the fact that they weren't there. He knew he had to live on their behalf. He still believed that they deserved to live more than he did but he would try to change that.

"Your body will hurt for a while, mostly because of your muscles. They were inactive for a while and being suspended like that also put a lot of pressure on your body, making your blood flow a bit difficult. You could've lost your arms if you had hung there any longer as the blood circulation was slowing down," the nurse said.

The thought of losing his arms shocked him. He would've been completely useless if that had happened. He already knew about his muscles but it didn't matter so much considering he would've been an invalid. He knew he'd regain his strength easily and soon he'd be back on his feet. He'd been through worse which made him grateful for the fact that he was found just in time.

"When will I be able to leave?" he asked.

Being in hospital reminded him of the last time he

was in hospital, and again he felt a pang of sadness that he was alone.

It had taken him months to work through the emotions he had felt all those years ago. Well, technically he hadn't worked through them. He had just learned how to push them down, and he could feel them slowly trying to come back to the surface the more aware he became. He couldn't allow his emotions to get the better of him though so he tried to push his memories to the side. He'd have to deal with them another day, or never, just like he had always done. He was never good at handling his emotions, even before Afghanistan. He wasn't a very emotional person, and he supposed it didn't do much good for him considering he was always having to deal with his past but he preferred to just ignore it, to push it down deep within him.

"We'd like to keep you here for a few more hours, but right now there is nothing that suggests anything major is wrong with you. We'll be giving you another drip just to make sure you are well hydrated again and then we'd like to do a few more tests on you just to confirm that everything is 100 percent alright before you get discharged," she replied. Sage knew better than to fight against hospital policy. He had tried that the last time he was in hospital. He had tried to fight his doctor when he wanted to leave. Being there was damaging him but he wasn't ready and they had to sedate him, so he knew he'd just have to wait it out this time around.

"Okay, I guess I'll just have to wait," he said. The nurse smiled and did a quick nod of her head, pleased with his answer. He wondered if she knew about his hospital track record, but she didn't seem worried either way.

"Good. I'll be back in a few hours to check in on you, until then just rest. Your body needs it." She turned her back and walked out of the room, closing the door behind her. He took note of the room, grateful for the fact that it was a private room so there weren't any empty beds for him to focus on. He tried his hardest to keep his mind busy and awake but soon he was fast asleep, and luckily for him, he was so high on pain killers his dreams didn't consist of anything frightening. Instead, he dreamed of Mia.

What felt like only minutes later, Sage was woken up by the click of the door opening. He didn't know how long he had slept for but when he saw the nurse's face coming into view, he realized it must have been a few hours. She held another bag of liquid in her hands.

"How are you feeling? Did you get some rest?" she asked as she checked his almost empty drip. He tried to sit up, wincing a bit as his body protested against him. He fought the urge to lay back down and forced himself to sit up as straight as possible. He knew he'd have to walk soon so he had to get used to the pain.

"I feel well-rested but is there anything I can take for the pain?" he asked. The painkillers had worn off during his sleep. He didn't want to come off weak and childlike but he knew he would need a little help just to get through walking. He could only imagine how much that would hurt compared to just sitting up. He really didn't want to get pushed out of the hospital in a wheelchair; that would be humiliating for an ex-army man.

"Don't worry, you'll be given something for the pain. It shouldn't last too long after you get moving and some proper food in your system," she smiled at him. At the mention of food, his stomach grumbled. He hadn't eaten in days and now that his body was getting liquids he started to feel a bit more normal and ready for food.

"Thank you, that's great. Is there any chance I could get some food?" he asked as she started changing his drip.

"Yes, of course. Once I've finished here I'll call someone to bring you a meal. It will be something small considering you haven't eaten in a few days," she said to him.

"That's perfectly fine. I'd eat anything at this point," he said with a laugh, his energy slowly coming back to him.

She finished attaching his new drip and immediately

left without a word. A few moments later another woman walked in with a tray of food in her hands. She placed the tray on his lap with a smile and left. It wasn't much, a small pile of mashed potatoes, a very pale and dull-looking chicken breast with a few baby carrots and some broccoli. Although it was all rather bland, Sage was grateful to finally get some food. He took his time eating and tried not to overdo it, leaving some on his plate. He knew he needed the food but he wouldn't risk his stomach going into cramps which was likely to happen if he overdid it so soon. He placed the half-eaten food on one of the bedside tables next to him and considered switching on the TV while he waited, but thought against it. He hadn't been much of a TV guy and he wouldn't start now just out of boredom.

He decided to spend the remainder of his time watching the drip slowly empty. It was boring and tedious but it distracted him nonetheless. He longed to leave. Within an hour his wish came true. The drip was empty and he could finally leave. The nurse came to do the final tests which all came back good. He slowly got out of bed. Standing took all of his energy as he felt a wave of dizziness go over him. He ignored it and pushed through as he had to leave and he wouldn't let anything stop him. Once on his feet, he took a few moments to stretch his body.

He flexed his muscles, ignoring the pain. He bent his

body this way and that way until he felt a little more mobile and able to walk. The nurse informed him that someone named Grier had been in to visit him while he was sleeping. He left a message for Sage letting him know he was in Florida, staying at the house using one of the studies while he was here and wished to see him when he was discharged. Sage headed straight for the house. There was no better place to be other than home, he thought. He was excited to get home. He just wanted to be comfortable in his own bed. Even after sleeping most of the day away, he was exhausted from moving already. He also wanted to have a shower and he wanted to see Mia but he knew he would have to talk to Grier before he did anything else.

Climbing into a cab outside the hospital Sage made his way to Grier. He made his way home with a sense of happiness at the thought. He didn't expect much from Grier, other than him just wanting to make sure he was okay. He soon arrived home and relief ran through his body as he looked at the place he called home in Florida. He climbed out of the cab and once he had paid the driver, he slowly made his way into the house. It wasn't hard to find the study Grier had claimed. He reached the door where he stood and knocked, waiting for permission to enter.

"Come in!" Grier shouted from the other side of the door. Sage opened the door and slowly walked in, trying not to wobble as he did so. Grier looked up from his computer and looked at Sage, a smile forming across his face. It was clear he was glad to see him.

"And so he lives!" he exclaimed as he got up and made his way over to him. "How are you feeling?" Grier asked as he gently laid a hand on his shoulder, giving it a soft squeeze. He didn't seem upset about what had happened. Hopefully because it was over now Sage wouldn't get a lecture about his actions.

"As good as I could be under the circumstances," Sage replied with a smile. Grier indicated to one of the seats in the study and Sage gratefully took it. His body needed to rest again.

"I'm sure, I'm sure! You're very fortunate," Grier said. Sage knew he was right. He had almost died and he only had one person to thank for making sure that hadn't happened. He just hadn't seen her yet.

"I'm truly grateful. I have a few people to thank, that's for sure," he replied. Grier nodded his head in agreement. Clearly not bothered about anything else but Sage's wellbeing.

"We're all happy that you're back and in one piece. It was a close call," Grier said. "We're still trying to figure out what is left of the Omens and how much of a threat they still have here but nothing is confirmed yet."

"Hopefully we can get rid of them once and for all. Their existence is causing a lot of trouble," Sage replied.

Just as Sage had finished his sentence the door swung open and both men turned to face who had interrupted their conversation. Mia stood frozen in the doorway looking at the two of them, holding a cup of what smelt like coffee as it wafted through the air. She clearly didn't expect Sage to be home already as she looked him over.

"Oh, I didn't realize you had company. I just came to bring you some coffee," she said as she entered the study, placing the coffee on the desk Grier had been using. Sage watched Mia as she walked into the small space. He wanted to thank her in private so he just smiled at her, hoping she could see the gratitude written on his face.

"I'm actually glad you're here, Mia. Please join us and take a seat," Grier said as he too smiled at her. Mia took a seat and looked from one man to the other as silence filled the room. She didn't know what to say to Sage especially in front of Grier. She wanted to ask him how he was but thought it better to wait until they were alone.

"Well," Grier said to them, breaking the silence at the same time, "I've been talking to Fiona a lot today and she is thoroughly impressed with how you managed to get our man back." Grier looked pointedly at Mia. "It showed a lot of strength and fire. You should be proud," he continued to say as she blushed at the compliment.

"Oh, thank you. Honestly, it wasn't anything really,"

she said trying to downplay all the effort she had put into getting Sage back. She knew she wouldn't have stopped trying to find him if she hadn't found him yesterday but they didn't need to know that. She would've searched the entire planet to get him back.

"Don't be so modest, Mia. Adam and I had a chat at length about exactly what you did, and the fact that you went with every lead not waiting to get told what to do was just great. You showed just how powerful you can be," Grier said.

"Yes, it was amazing. I have you to thank for being alive," Sage said to her, looking her straight in the eye. After a few seconds of holding each other's gaze, Mia had to look away. She couldn't risk Grier seeing the connection to Sage that she was sure was written all over her face.

"You're welcome. We're a team and I knew I couldn't just sit around and do nothing so honestly, I'm happy I could help," she replied.

"And it's because of that that after some discussion with Fiona we have come to the agreement that you will be made a Screaming Demon," Grier said with a triumphant smile. There hadn't been many female Screaming Demons before but Mia had earned it. Sage and Mia couldn't believe it. She stared at Grier in shock as did Sage. After everything that had gone wrong because of her, she hadn't thought anything would make her worthy of being a Screaming Demon but she was chuffed.

"Wow, I'm speechless. That's such an honor. Thank you so much," Mia said as the words tumbled out of her mouth in a rush of excitement.

"I agree. That is amazing," Sage said. He didn't believe he deserved it like Mia did.

"You've both shown a lot of fight and so you deserve it. Just don't let us down," Grier joked but they both knew he was serious.

"Now that that's done, I need to finish up some work before I head back home." His hint getting across to both Sage and Mia as they got to their feet and left the study.

2

---

ia couldn't believe the news she had just gotten. Being made a Screaming Demon was such an honor and she wanted to jump up and down with joy. She knew if she had to do it all again, she would in a heartbeat. It wasn't about getting some sort of title or label. She hadn't thought about that or cared about it either when she had gone looking for Sage. She just knew that she had to save him no matter what. When she had been wrapped up in helping to find him she just constantly remembered the time he had saved her from an angry Omen, how he had come out of nowhere and saved her. She owed Sage her life for that night. He had constantly saved her or helped her in some way and there was no way she would've been able to live with herself if she hadn't done everything in her power to find Sage. It wasn't just because she loved him but it was also because she could see how much of an impact he had made in everyone's life and he deserved a chance.

She also wanted him to have a chance so he could eventually let her in. Maybe it was selfish but she wanted to be selfish with him. She wanted to show him that she could look after him if he let her. She was a stronger and better person, better than she had ever been before, and she felt as if she could change someone's life now. She didn't feel like she was just drifting along the wave of life anymore. She had made something of herself.

Sage and Mia stood outside the study door for a while before either of them said a thing. Both of them were thinking of the honor Mia had just received. She felt undeserving of it. She hadn't done anything to deserve being called a Screaming Demon. She had almost ruined everything with her actions. But Sage knew Mia deserved it. Unlike him. He had fought an Omen and had gotten himself kidnapped. That wasn't what Screaming Demons did. He felt disappointed in himself for what he had caused. Perhaps they should strip away his right to be a Demon.

They could both feel the electric energy that pulsed between them. It was undeniable but they both ignored it. It was a strange feeling for them and they honestly didn't know how to take it. They hadn't seen each other properly in days.

"I just wanted to thank you personally for everything you did, Mia. I'm in debt to you for saving my life," Sage said, breaking the silence. He knew just a simple thank you would never be enough to truly show how grateful he was to her, but it was all he could do at that moment. He couldn't do much else considering he was still so weak. He had thought about hugging her but thought against it. Not only was his body too sore for that kind of action but he also didn't think it would be right. He still had a lot to think about with regards to Mia and he didn't want to act on impulse. He could see the bags under her eyes. The more he looked at her, it was clear she hadn't been sleeping much and he couldn't under-stand why. Was it because of him, he wondered. Had she lost sleep because he was missing? He didn't want to believe it though.

Mia looked at him, taking him in. He looked better, healthier than the last time she had seen him. She invol-untarily shivered at the memory of him just a day ago. It was a memory she would never forget. She would always remember how she had heard him cry when she found him.

He was still skinnier than normal although he had more of a healthy glow about him. His eyes were sunken in a bit with blueish black circles around them and he still looked a bit battered and beaten but nevertheless, he was alright and home. She could see the look in his eyes, the look of gratitude that was written on his face. It made her heart leap in her chest.

She had left him at the hospital in the early hours of the morning, unsure if he'd be happy that she was there in bed with him. She had stayed long enough to make sure he was alright. She had kept her hand on his chest, feeling his heartbeat under her hand until she had fallen asleep for a while next to him. She had headed back to the house to make sure Grier had a working space while he was visiting. He had stayed at a hotel during the night while Mia was at the hospital with Sage. He hadn't asked any questions about it and Mia was thankful for that.

She wanted to wrap her arms around Sage again but stopped herself. She knew she couldn't do that. She was unsure if he even remembered her holding him when he was out of the well. He had been so out of it due to dehydration.

"Your life matters, Sage. Of course, I would've made sure you came home," she said softly, avoiding his gaze. It was just too much for her to handle. She didn't want to come across as gooey and vulnerable but she also wanted to be honest with him. She couldn't tell him she loved him as much as the words were on the tip of her tongue, at risk of stumbling out into the open between them. If she told Sage she loved him, it could change everything and she wasn't sure if things would change for the better or not.

She had to force herself to remember what had happened days before he went missing. He had pulled away from her so she didn't doubt that would continue now that he was back. She couldn't allow herself to think that her saving his life meant anything more than that. It didn't mean he would all of a sudden love her too. The thought was unrealistic and Mia had to push it out of her mind.

"Is there anything you'd like to have for dinner?" she asked as a way to change the topic. She could at least distract herself with cooking, she needed to get a lot of distance between herself and her thoughts. She also needed some distance from Sage.

"You really don't have to go to the effort for me," Sage said. As much as she wanted to help him get back on his feet, she knew cooking would be for herself more than it would be for him, despite the end result being whatever he wanted.

"Really, just choose something. You need a good home-cooked meal now that you're safe," she said. She knew he needed a few home-cooked meals to fully regain his strength but dinner would be a start.

"Um, okay, spaghetti bolognese would be great," he replied after a few minutes of thinking. Thankfully Mia loved pasta so it was a good choice and as much as she loved to eat it she also loved to cook it.

"Okay, perfect. Spaghetti bolognese it is," Mia said. She knew if she wanted it to be good it would at least take some time for everything to cook so she could distract herself happily for a while.

"If you don't mind I'm going to go lay down for a while," Sage said. She could tell he was exhausted. She could see a few beads of sweat forming on his forehead. It was obviously taking a lot of his energy to stand and she also knew he had to be in some sort of pain while his body still recovered. She could only imagine what he was going through.

"No problem. Shall I wake you up when dinner is ready?" she asked.

"That would be great. Thank you," he said.

And with that, Sage headed for his bedroom while Mia headed for the kitchen.

Mia spent some time getting everything she needed out and laid them before her. Slowly, she started putting everything together, chopping the fresh garlic and carrots, so she could create a fantastic meal for the two of them. Just because there was nothing romantic going on between them, didn't mean they shouldn't eat a great meal, she thought. She cooked away, silently humming to herself as she worked, trying not to think too much about Sage and how he might be feeling.

"Something smells delicious."

Mia turned to see Grier standing in the doorway of the kitchen, holding his overnight bag and his laptop bag. Clearly he was ready to leave. She had almost completely forgotten he was there at all because he had stayed in the study most of the time.

"You're more than welcome to stay for dinner," Mia offered. She wasn't sure if there would be enough for all of them because she had only had herself and Sage on her mind but if he did stay she'd make a plan so he would get a plate.

"No, no, that's quite alright. I better head home to my family," he replied. Mia was jealous of Grier. He had a family and she didn't. She just had someone she loved who would push her away almost every chance he got, not much of a family.

"Of course, thank you so much for coming all this way," she said. Although he had only managed to arrive after Mia had found Sage she was still grateful he had taken time out to come to Florida in the first place. She knew he would've done it anyway considering he was the boss but she also knew she had taken the situation into her own hands which could've ended badly.

"I'm glad you called. Don't ever hesitate to call if you need anything," Grier said. She knew she was capable of doing a lot on her own so she wasn't sure if she'd call him for help, but more just to inform him of what she was doing. She was after all a Screaming Demon now which held a lot more power than just a Hell Kat.

"Thank you, I appreciate that. Let me show you out," she said as she led him to the door. She showed him out and watched as he got into the cab that was already waiting outside, he had clearly called the cab company before he had stopped to say goodbye. She waved him off and turned back to the kitchen, she couldn't risk the food burning since it was almost done. She gave the bolognese one last taste before adding one last pinch of salt. She drained the pasta, rinsing it, and then mixed it in with the bolognese. She found it was much easier to dish up that way.

Everything was cooked and ready so Mia decided she would set the dining room table before she went to wake Sage up from his nap. She was impressed with herself as she looked at the table once more. Anyone would be lucky to come home to a meal like this she thought and yet she had cooked a meal for someone who would probably go back to acting as if she didn't exist in a few days. It had been just over an hour and she felt if he slept any longer he may not be able to sleep later that evening.

Sage woke up when he heard a gentle yet loud enough tapping on his bedroom door. She didn't want to startle him by just walking into his room.

"Sage? Dinner is ready," Mia said softly from the

other side of the door. She didn't enter which Sage appreciated. He didn't want to be seen so vulnerable and small in his bed.

"Thank you," he said, a bit dazed as he slowly woke up. "I'll be out in a minute," he replied. Mia went back to the kitchen, wanting to make sure everything looked presentable. It was Sage's first proper meal since he got out of the well so she wanted it to be the best meal he could have.

Sage lay in bed for a while before he stretched his body. This time it didn't hurt so much and he was grateful. He knew he just needed the rest so his body could get back to its normal self and heal from the inside out. He decided to have a quick shower before going for dinner. Obviously he had been cleaned up while in hospital but he still felt dirty after everything.

"I'm just going to have a shower and then I'll be right there," he called out to Mia, hoping she could hear him. He wasn't sure if she was waiting outside his door or not for a reply from him.

He switched on the hot water and waited for the bathroom to steam up as he always did. Once he was satisfied with the amount of steam that hung in the air he climbed into the shower. He stood still under the showerhead, allowing the fresh hot water to rush over him. He smiled to himself. He never realized just how much he could miss having a shower but when he was getting covered in dirty cold water just days before it was obvious that fresh water was so much better. His body almost melted with pleasure. He would never take showering for granted ever again.

He washed every inch of himself, making sure to scrub at his skin until it was red and raw. He had been covered in dirt, urine and feces for two days which brought him a sense of shame and disgust. He felt as if he would never truly be clean again after that but that didn't mean he couldn't try. He washed himself twice, making sure he could be as clean as possible. He wanted to bathe in a tub full of disinfectant. He remembered how Mia had hugged him when she found him and he shuddered at the thought. He couldn't imagine what she thought of him finding him like she had. He would've been disgusted at the sight. He stepped out of the shower and changed into his own clothes considering the hospital had given him scrubs to wear. His clothes had been chucked away and there hadn't been anything else for him to wear. He felt almost himself again as he walked to the dining room to meet Mia for dinner.

"I'm sorry for the wait. I just wanted to shower quickly," he said, when he saw her sitting at the table sipping a glass of water. He still wasn't sure if Mia had heard him the first time.

"Don't worry, that's alright. I'm sure it felt good," she replied. He took a look at the table. He was impressed with how much effort she had put into it all. The table was set, with the food in a serving bowl in the middle. He hadn't had any of Mia's cooking before and as his senses took over him the wonderful smell of food was almost too much. It took everything inside of him not to shove his face into the bowl filled with spaghetti bolognese which Mia had already mixed. He took a seat across from Mia as she offered him something to drink.

"Just some water please." He couldn't help but feel like royalty with the treatment Mia was giving him. He wasn't sure he deserved it after what he had put her through before the kidnapping and he felt guilty. She didn't seem to mind giving him the attention as she placed a glass in front of him and poured some iced water into it with a gentle smile.

"How are you feeling?" Mia asked as she took a seat after pouring him some water. She didn't want to baby him but she also didn't expect him to do everything on his own. She was okay with taking on the responsibility of helping him for a few days, just to make sure he didn't strain himself. She knew he was a strong man but everyone needed help now and again when they weren't able to help themselves.

"I'm feeling much better after my nap. My body doesn't feel 100 percent itself yet but I'm sure it'll be back on track in no time," he replied. Mia was pleased to hear such a positive attitude from Sage, she would probably still be a wreck if the roles were reversed.

"I'm so glad to hear that. It must have been a lot to go through," she said as she tiptoed around the topic gently, not wanting to make it obvious that she wanted to talk about it. She was desperate to know how he had been throughout the experience, he hadn't said much about it at all which for Mia was strange. Most people wanted to talk about their trauma, but Sage ignored it. She noticed that was a pattern of his, ignoring things around him.

"It was," he stated, not leaving much room for the topic to go any further. It wasn't enough for Mia.

"You know, you can talk about it if you want. You don't have to keep it all inside to deal with alone. I'm here for you," she said gently while she looked into his blue eyes. The feeling of love for him oozed out of her every pore. She could almost physically see it reach across the table and touch him, but luckily it was just her imagination.

"I know I can talk about it but I just don't want to," he said sternly. He always worked through things his own way and in his own time. He didn't need help from anyone. Actually, he knew that wasn't entirely true considering what had happened to him when he had been so helpless but he knew he didn't have to talk about it, especially to Mia. If she knew how weak he had felt and how he had almost wished for death he knew she would think less of him and he didn't want her to think any less of him than she already did. He knew she must've lost whatever respect she had for him when he had been so cruel to her so he could only imagine how much respect she'd have for him if she knew what he went through.

"You could look into therapy if you don't want to talk to me," she suggested. Although she wanted to be the one to help him, she knew there were other options.

"I don't need to talk to some shrink about my feelings. I don't need someone to give me drugs or coping mechanisms to work with," he said irritated. He wished she would just drop the topic, but she didn't.

"No one says you have to take any drugs, Sage, but I don't think it's healthy to just let everything boil inside," she said.

"Mia, do you not think I went through therapy when I left the army? Do you think it helped? It didn't. Nothing can change what has already happened and there's no need for me to harp on about it," he said. He knew that although he hadn't spoken about what had happened to him, everyone knew he had been the only survivor.

"I'm sure you did and maybe it didn't help then but it could be good if you go again," she replied.

"If it didn't work for me then, what makes you think it would work for me now?" he said.

"We could look into a different kind of therapy. Something that could make you feel more alive. It doesn't have to be the typical therapy everyone goes to," she said.

"I appreciate the thought, Mia, I really do, but I'd really like to just leave it alone if you don't mind," he replied sternly. Mia decided to drop the subject, knowing no matter what she said he wouldn't change his mind.

They proceeded to eat dinner in silence, both not wanting to say anything to the other that could make the conversation any worse than it already was. The air around them was tense as they avoided eye contact.

Once Sage had finished his plate of food, he looked at Mia as she stared vacantly at her plate while she ate. He was grateful for everything she had done for him but he knew there was no way he would talk to her or anyone else for that matter about what was going on in his head. He was strong enough to deal with it on his own.

"Thank you for dinner, it was delicious," he said as Mia finished her plate. She was a slow eater he noted.

"It was my pleasure," she smiled at him, although it didn't really reach her eyes. He had hurt her feelings like he always did, although this time he hadn't meant to.

"If you don't mind, I'm going to head back to bed," he said as he pushed his chair back so he could stand, feeling a pinch of pain shoot through his legs as he stood. He held his facial expression together, not wanting to give his pain away. He really hoped that by the time he woke up the next morning the pain would be nonexistent, he needed to get his strength back but it would be hard if he continued to be in pain.

"That's quite alright," she replied, "you need your rest." She didn't fight him. She had already lost every battle with him so there was no point trying anymore.

"Thank you. Would you like some help cleaning up?" he asked.

"Oh no, don't worry about it. I'll take care of it," she said. Sage stared at her as she smiled with reassurance.

"Okay then, well, goodnight," he said. He turned and headed for his room once again.

Mia cleaned the dishes, taking her time cleaning the rest of the kitchen as well. She knew it had been a traumatic experience for Sage and she wished she could help him but he was stern when he said he didn't want any help and so she decided it would be better if she just left the topic alone. She hoped that if he needed her he'd go to her when he was ready but she knew that was highly unlikely. Once the kitchen was spotless and everything was packed away neatly, Mia made her way to her room where she showered and got into bed. She was also exhausted from the last few days. She hadn't realized how much of a toll it had taken on her until her head hit the pillow and she fell asleep happy knowing Sage was at home, just a few feet away from her.

*Sage stood in the hallway with a handful of packets filled with groceries with his back toward Mia.*

*"What are you doing?" Mia asked. Sage, however, didn't move. He didn't respond to Mia at all. She walked around him so she could see his face. When she took a closer look she noticed he didn't have much of a facial expression. He stared vacantly ahead as if he was seeing something she couldn't.*

*"Sage, are you okay?" she asked with concern laced in her voice.*

*He finally registered her voice as his eyes focused on her face, a smile forming across his lips.*

*"Hi, yeah, sorry I got distracted there," he replied. Mia looked into the direction he was previously facing, wondering if there was anything there. She noticed nothing.*

*"What were you looking at?" she asked.*

*"Weirdly enough, I was looking into the future," he said. Mia couldn't understand what he meant.*

*"What do you mean? Can you see the future now?" she asked teasingly.*

*"Haha," he laughed, "nothing like that, silly. It's like I came into the house and I could picture myself doing this for the rest of my life. I could picture myself coming home with shopping, coming home to you and this house," he said as he looked around. Mia reached forward and took the shopping*

*from his hands and put them on the ground. She wrapped her arms around him and hugged him tightly.*

*"I can picture that too," she replied, the thought of their future making her smile.*

Mia continued to dream of her and Sage, she couldn't help her subconscious from making them an item in her mind. She smiled to herself while she slept, thinking of Sage.

## 3

The next day Mia woke up well-rested. She knew that her vision of a future with Sage was just a dream and she wished for the dreams to stop since there was no future between them. It hurt her to think about the fact that she had to live with someone who constantly made it obvious that he didn't want her. It was a saddening thought for her because she wanted him more and more every day.

She knew the odds of that happening were slim since Sage had made no move toward her. He had barely looked at her the previous day besides their conversation. She had no control over her mind when she slept and the ones that were harder to think about were the dreams she had of having him, the ones where he loved her and wanted her too. It pulled at her heart the more she thought about it. She longed for him but she knew she couldn't have him which made it harder for her.

Mia walked to Sage's room to check in on him, wanting to make sure he had had something to eat and to her surprise, she found it empty. She didn't want to panic immediately because the odds of him disappearing so soon after coming home seemed unlikely, so she walked around the house and thankfully found Sage in the yard working out. She could tell he had lost some weight so he was clearly eager to get it all back. She wished he would take some more time to rest though. His body had been through so much and she honestly didn't think he was 100 percent ready to be working out so soon. She could understand that he was an army man and that he had the constant need to feel powerful and strong but he could've rested for one more day before starting to work out again.

Mia stood silently watching Sage from inside the house. She watched as his muscles flexed and sweat started to form over various parts of his visible skin. She watched him push himself and she could see the frustration on his face as his body resisted some of the work. She could see a few pained looks as he continued to work out. She felt sorry for him, and a bit guilty. She wished that she had found him sooner; if she had, he wouldn't be so broken. She knew she had done the best she could but she had waited an extra day and if she had just searched for him the minute she realized he was gone, maybe he wouldn't be so weak and so traumatized.

She decided to change into some of her workout clothes so she could join him. She knew that as a Screaming Demon she would have to have a bit more muscle to her if anything else happened and a part of her just wanted to be close to him. She wanted to keep a close eye on him all the time, in case he ever needed her but was too afraid to ask directly. She didn't bother joining in on Sage's workout though. She knew it would be too hard for her so she did her own a little bit away from him. As much as she wanted to be near him she was also worried about their conversation from the night before. She wasn't sure if he was still upset with her for pushing too much about the therapy. She had just wanted to help him. He didn't say anything when she joined him in the yard so it was clear to her that he was still upset like she thought but even though he didn't say anything he didn't move away from her either so she stood her ground as she worked out alongside him.

She decided to do basic core strengthening exercises and body weighted exercises. She hadn't exactly been working out much before and she also didn't spend much time in a gym so to her that was enough to make her strong and fit.

There wasn't much space for them to work out as there had been a storm overnight which had caused a few branches to fall all over the yard, disrupting the space they had. The branches lay scattered across the yard. It looked extremely beautiful as well as destructive. Mia decided to take it upon herself to start clearing some of the branches away so they could have more space and so the yard looked better. After putting a pair of gloves on from the garden shed she started picking up as many branches as she could and carried them to the outside bin. It didn't take long for Sage to quietly join in to help her. They were both slowly picking up branches and moving them, moving around each other without saying a word. With an arm full of branches in her arms Mia turned around and bumped into Sage, dropping the branches at their feet from the impact.

"Sorry," she said sheepishly, staring into his eyes. He didn't say a word but continued to stare back at her. The longer Mia stared at Sage the more she could see something burn beneath his eyes, a look that almost drew her closer to him. She could tell Sage wanted her just as much as she wanted him and yet he didn't move. It annoyed her the longer it went on and within a second he turned his back on her, continuing the job of picking up branches.

"Agh!" she huffed in annoyance. "I'm getting tired of this," she said as she ripped off the gloves and threw them on the ground. She walked past him, kicking branches out of her way. She was extremely irritated with Sage's attitude. She couldn't take the silent treatment anymore, especially since she had just been trying to help him.

She was almost inside when she heard a groan come from Sage behind her. She turned to face him to see he had already started walking toward her. Soon she was running to her room, Sage close behind her, and in no time at all they were outside her bedroom. They stood there panting, staring at each other for a while, neither of them breaking their gaze as the fire within started to burn to a fever pitch.

Sage couldn't take it anymore. When Mia had joined him outside, it was bad enough that she looked so hot in her tight workout clothes and when he watched her stretch her body beside him the fire in him lit up immediately. He wanted her and when she had bumped into him he tried to pull away, he tried to stop himself but when he had looked into her eyes he could tell she wanted him just as much and then he couldn't stop himself. He went after her as she ran to her room. He loved the chase but didn't want to play games either. He yearned for her.

Her door was closed and before she could reach for the handle, Sage had his arms around her, her body pressed against her door while he turned her to face him and just like that his mouth was on hers, their lips pressed together desperately wanting each other. Mia could feel the need Sage had for her as his hands traveled over her body, wanting to touch every part of her. Mia let her hands explore his body too, feeling his sweaty body beneath her fingertips.

Their mouths opened, inviting their tongues to dance with desire, tasting each other as they both moaned with pleasure and need. Sage reached for the handle behind Mia without removing his lips from hers and soon the door was pushed open while their bodies tumbled into the room. Their hands were reaching for skin, fumbling as they kept their eyes closed and mouths glued to each other, neither of them wanting to be free. Sage, unwillingly, freed his lips so he could trail them down Mia's neck, kissing her exposed skin, moving his way down from her neck to her shoulder, and across her collarbone, while his hands reached for the bottom of her top as he tugged it up and over her head. Mia followed his lead and reached for the bottom of his shirt, throwing it across the room once it was off him. Their hands reached for each other, grabbing at each other's half-exposed bodies. Mia had her hands on his back while Sage had his hands wrapped around her hair, pulling her closer to him.

The need and want for each other had been burning in both of them for so long that they both just wanted the other to be naked as quickly as possible. Their breathing echoed throughout the room.

Sage's hands hungrily removed her bra. Desperate to feel her, he cupped her breasts as he went and she whimpered under his touch. He took a moment to look her over, savoring the way she looked as her eyes were filled with lust. His hands moved up the side of her body and found their way into her hair once more as his mouth found hers again and groaned as their lips touched. Her arms were wrapped around his neck as her body pressed against his. Her chest pressed against him, she felt the heat of his body against hers and she moaned as excitement filled her body. They made their way to her bed, still connected to each other as they slowly stepped in the direction of the bed, and as their knees felt the edge bump against their skin, they collapsed onto the bed, Sage on top of Mia. He reached for the band of her pants and tugged them off of her revealing her underwear. She lay still on the bed as her breathing picked up while he looked at her. He had gotten off the bed and was standing just at the edge of it. Mia could see his member pressed against his pants. She sat up and tugged his pants off as he stood there, both only in their underwear.

Mia pulled Sage back onto the bed and found her way on top of him. She felt a pang of sadness as she saw the bruises on his wrists, ankles and around his rib cage from being hung in the well. She wanted to kiss every area of his body but the longing they had both been carrying inside them over the past few weeks was stronger than gentle kisses, it was more passionate, more desperate than that. There wasn't time to be gentle though as Sage reached for Mia, flipping her onto her back as he tugged her underwear off. She gasped in shock but she was ready and wanting, she was ready for Sage. He squeezed her ass as his hands worked their way around her back and he placed himself between her legs, still with his underwear on. He pressed his hips against her, teasing her.

"Do you have any condoms in here?" he asked against her skin as he kissed her neck, sending a wave of goose-bumps across her body.

"Yes, in the drawer," she breathed as she turned her head to the drawer she meant. Sage reached over, opening the drawer and took a condom. In one quick motion he had ripped it open, pulled off his underwear and placed it on so he could take his place in between her legs once more.

He bent over her, kissing and sucking on her neck as he lowered his hips. She moaned as he met her while she wrapped her arms around his neck pulling him closer to her. He placed his arms under her back, cradling her body as he pressed himself against her while his hips moved. He groaned against her skin, overwhelmed with pleasure as their bodies melted into each other. Mia closed her eyes and tilted her head back, giving herself completely to Sage. She could feel his need for her and she lived for it, feeding off it as her body reached its limit. She moaned as she let go, followed by Sage who tensed and then relaxed on top of her.

He lifted himself off of her and lay next to her on his side. He placed an arm over her naked body so he could turn her onto her side, his chest pressed against her back as he held her tightly against his body. He could feel her heart beat against his arms as he wrapped his arms around her chest. He listened to her breathing as it slowed down next to him. He loved the feeling of her body against his. It brought him a sense of peace he hadn't experienced before. He felt renewed almost.

4

Sage lay next to Mia, feeling her skin next to his sent a rush of warmth through his body. A sense of tenderness went through him, and another feeling he hadn't felt for a very long time, a feeling he thought he'd never feel again.

A part of him knew it was time to let go of his guilt toward Laura. He couldn't change the fact that she was gone. All he could do was realize what he did have and that was Mia. He was still terrified of loving again. The thought of loving another person was almost overwhelming to think about. He had never gotten over losing the first love of his life and he didn't want to risk experiencing that again. He knew it would be harder on him if anything happened to Mia. She had already done so much for him that he knew he loved her more than he had ever loved before. If he allowed himself to love her, he would have to protect her as much as he could. He would kill someone for her and that thought was shocking to him. He'd never felt like that before but Mia was the best thing that had happened to him in a long time and she proved herself over and over again.

He ran his hand over her arm, noticing her skin was as smooth as he remembered. She sighed at his touch, sparking a rush of excitement through Sage. He couldn't help it, she sounded content and yet so sexy. His hands started to explore her body and soon she had herself twisted around so she could see him, and as their eyes met, so did their mouths. It didn't take long for another condom to be pulled out of the drawer. Their bodies sang with pleasure, but this time it wasn't as needy as the time before. They savored each other's bodies, taking it slowly as they touched each other with passion. Their bodies hot with desire as Sage moved himself inside of Mia. They again collapsed into a pile of hot and sweaty bodies. The sex felt better every time.

As they lay next to each other, finding their normal breathing patterns, Sage knew it was possible that he could love Mia. She had shown such bravery when it came to finding him, he knew she must've gone through hell making sure she found who had taken him. She was a strong and courageous woman, and he couldn't deny that he found it extremely sexy and attractive. When he had been in that well, he had thought about her so much. He had wished he could've gotten the chance to be with her and now while she lay in his arms he knew he would give in.

He had pictured them together and he couldn't deny that a feeling inside of him was longing for that to be true. He knew she was able to look after herself and yet she also put herself in danger most of the time but he felt like he could take care of her, he could make sure that no one brought her any danger. He knew he was strong enough for that. He also knew that she would bring some adventure back into his life and he knew he needed that after everything he had been through. Adventure would be good for him. She would be good for him.

He was surprised by the rush of emotions he felt. He had tried his hardest to push them away since he had met her but it was getting harder for him to deny his true feelings. He knew it wouldn't be long until he would have to say something, but he knew it wasn't the right time yet. So he wrapped himself around her body and drifted off to sleep.

*"Sage?" a voice called from behind him. All the hairs on the back of his neck lifted at the sound of the voice. He knew who it was and he was terrified to turn and face it.*

*"It's okay. I'm not here to cause any problems," the voice said, sensing his mood. He slowly turned to face the voice and he was met by Laura, a smile across her face.*

Sage knew he was dreaming. There was nothing around them besides whiteness.

"Where are we?" he asked her.

"We're nowhere and everything in between," she replied as she shrugged, letting her arms fall to her sides. Sage looked around him and he could agree that they were nowhere.

"Why are we here?" he asked her, nothing made sense to him.

"You tell me, you called me here," she stated. Was he dead? He couldn't remember dying though so that seemed highly unlikely.

"What do you mean I called you here?" he couldn't understand what she meant.

"We're here because you need to talk to me and so here I am, talking to you," she said. A part of him still didn't understand but then a light went off in his head. He knew why she was there in his dream. It was his way of finally letting her go.

"We both knew this day was going to come sooner or later," she continued as she watched his face change.

"I suppose so," he replied. It seemed so real to him. He knew when he woke up it would have only been a dream but he took the opportunity to talk to her once and for all.

"You look good," he said, noticing how she wasn't in her usual state. She wasn't covered in blood or dirt, there was no evidence of her dying at all.

"Thank you. So do you," she said with a smile.

*"You know I really did love you," he stated, wanting her to hear it one last time.*

*"I know you did." She smiled at him.*

*Sage wasn't sure how much time he had left and so he started to ramble.*

*"You're gone now though and I've been holding on for so long, thinking that I'd be betraying you if I moved on but I can't think like that anymore. You're not here and I can't change that. I have to let you go. I have to let you go so I can love again," he said. She smiled at him knowingly, not inter-rupting him as he laid it all out in front of them.*

*"You deserve all the happiness in the world, Sage, and probably more than that. I wasn't easy to love, I know that, but I was grateful for the time we had. It meant the world to me and if I could change how our paths worked out, I would, but we both know that's not possible and so I don't want to hold you back any longer. It's okay to let me go," she said as she took his hands into hers.*

*"It feels like I'm replacing you though," he replied.*

*"I'm no longer with you, Sage, so you're not replacing me because there is no me to replace," she said.*

*"But we didn't get the chance to say goodbye," he said.*

*"Say what you need to say now and then let yourself be free," she replied. A part of Sage's subconscious knew that this was his way of letting her go so he could move on and although he knew it wasn't real, he decided to go with it,*

*saying the things he wished he'd had the chance to say before losing Laura.*

*"Well, I want you to know that I will always cherish what we had. You were the first woman I truly loved and I will always be grateful for you. You allowed me to feel in a way I didn't think I could. I'm so sorry we never got the chance to have more. God knows I would've given you the world if I could've," he said, feeling a release within as he accepted his past could be put behind him.*

*"Thank you, Sage," was all Laura said as she slowly started to disappear in front of him, leaving him alone in his dream as it quickly changed scenes.*

When Sage woke up halfway through the night with his body curved around Mia he felt a feeling of love growing stronger in his chest. He knew the dream with Laura hadn't been real but a part of him felt like it was what he needed to move on. As much as he could never truly tell Laura all those things in person, he felt that on a spiritual level he could let her go so he could move on with his life. He didn't want to push Mia away anymore. He felt like he was ready to let her in. He pulled her closer to him and fell back to sleep, a sleep that didn't consist of any bad dreams, a sleep that was empty and peaceful, something he hadn't experienced in a long time.

5

Sage and Mia stayed wrapped up in their own world for a few days, getting to know each other more. They laughed and joked around, spending their waking hours constantly at each other's side. Sage started to love Mia more than he thought he would the more time he spent with her. He got to learn what made her laugh, and what irritated her. He had tried so hard not to let her in, and the closer she got to him the more he wondered why. She was an amazing and beautiful woman, everything he had ever wanted.

Sage knew he needed a few days to get his strength back and being with Mia made it that much better once he had opened himself up to the possibility of them being together. They hadn't heard from anyone besides a few calls from Grier just checking in on Sage and they appreciated the alone time they got. There was a part of him that wanted to take Mia away, away from every-thing, and start a new life with her. He loved being a part of the Screaming Demons but he wanted a better life for Mia, something that wasn't so dangerous. He had watched how she continued to try to make herself into a stronger person and he couldn't help but feel like it was his fault. He had turned her into someone who had to constantly make sure she could handle whatever came her way. He knew it wasn't really all his fault. She had joined the Hell Kats on her own but he still felt like it was a simpler time before they moved to Florida and as much as he loved the life they had, he couldn't help but constantly be aware of the danger that came at them from all sides most of the time.

Sage would spend a few hours in the yard working out every day. He was sleeping better, eating more and he wanted to regain his muscles as quickly as possible. He didn't like feeling weak. He even noticed that Mia was stronger than him in some ways which turned him on greatly. He couldn't get over how sexy she looked pretty much all the time.

While they were having lunch Mia's phone went off, their world vanishing as Mia took note of the number on her screen, a look of concern on her face. Sage couldn't imagine who it could be but he knew it must've been important.

"Hey, what's up?" Mia said into the phone. She wasn't

official with her answer but Sage could hear the seriousness in her voice. Whoever was on the phone was clearly someone Mia knew.

Sage had no idea who it could be. He didn't want to seem nosey so he hadn't paid attention to the name that had appeared. He trusted Mia so he let her handle business.

The person on the line started talking. Sage could hear a faint voice rambling from the other end. The person was talking quick, the message was urgent.

"Okay, cool. Thanks for letting me know. We'll be down there to check it out as soon as possible," Mia said and then hung up.

She turned to Sage who had been watching her throughout her conversation, "We have to go to the club," she said.

"Why, what's going on?" he asked. He couldn't make out anything when she had been on the phone so he was clueless.

"Apparently a woman has been coming around the club lately. No one knows who she is so they're all a bit concerned," she replied.

Sage knew that strange people always meant trouble, and he also knew that nothing could go wrong like it had not so long ago.

"That doesn't sound so good, let's go." Mia nodded her head in agreement. Within a few minutes, they were both out of the door and on their way to the club, both worried about the potential problem that could be on their hands.

They couldn't trust anyone and they knew that if anything they couldn't let anyone hang around the club that didn't belong there. The last time that happened, Sage went missing and almost died and if this unknown woman had anything to do with the Omens that could only mean things could get worse.

Once they got to the club they were both greeted by hugs and cheers from everyone there. The Hell Kats were proud of Mia for her hard work as well as the Screaming Demons. They were all happy that Sage had been brought back to them and they also knew about them both being made Screaming Demons. The entire club went crazy for them. They were welcomed back like they were long lost family and Mia's heart sang with happiness at the idea. She felt like her life mattered while she was with the Screaming Demons and she felt proud of the life she had started to build for herself. She had started painting more and the longer she spent time around Sage the more she was sure he was starting to fall for her like she had for him.

"Shots for everyone, on the house!" Mike shouted. Mia smiled at him. It was thanks to him and the video footage that Mia was even able to get a lead on Sage's whereabouts.

Mike poured a long row of shots for everyone, and soon they were all cheering as they swung the shots back. It didn't take long before drinks were going around and the music was filling the air with a good atmosphere. The woman was nowhere to be seen and so Mia and Sage decided to enjoy themselves while they were there. They hadn't been out in public in a few days and it felt good to be out of the house for a while, although they loved their little world it was always good being around people who cared about them.

"Mia!" called one of the Hell Kats. "Why don't you give us and Sage a show? You were so good the last time," she said with a wink. Mia blushed at the idea but soon all the Hell Kats were cheering her on, pushing her to give Sage a lap dance. Sage met eyes with Mia and shrugged. There was nothing he could do to help her.

"Come on, ladies, I'm sure not everyone wants to see that," Mia said, trying her luck to dismiss the idea. It didn't work; soon the whole club was cheering her on too.

"Okay, okay," she said as she buckled to the pressure. With the way things were between her and Sage, she didn't mind spicing things up a bit.

She walked over to a chair and placed it in the center of the dance floor. She then took Sage by the hand and placed him on the chair in front of her. Although they had had sex just a few days before, the sexual tension between them could be cut with a knife. Soon the whole club could see it and they watched as Mia slowly started her dance for Sage.

She placed herself behind him, trailing her tongue up his neck to his ear. He shivered at her touch. He wanted to touch her but fought against it. She twirled around the chair, landing on her feet, shoulder-width apart in front of him, her back to him as she swung her hips in a taunting manner as her hands traveled up her body and into her hair. She bent from the waist and stretched her hands to the floor, shifting her weight to her one leg as she ran her hand up her leg toward her hip where she stopped as she looked over her shoulder and looked at Sage, noticing how he licked his lips with desire. She lost herself in her movements, only slightly aware of her body moving closer to Sage until she was on his lap, facing him. She pressed her body against his as she ran her fingers up into his hair.

Sage watched Mia, completely captivated by her body and the way it moved. Her performance took him back to the first night they had sex in the back office and a part of him wanted to do it again as she pressed herself against him, taunting him. She was zoned out, completely focused on moving her body and touching him, teasing him. The longer it went on the more Sage couldn't take it. He grabbed her hand and pulled her outside, the club going wild behind them. Sage didn't care. He wanted Mia and that was all he could think about.

He pulled her body against a wall as they became covered in darkness. His lips on hers, opening her mouth with his tongue as the hunger for her grew in his chest. She moaned as she wrapped her fingers around his hair once more, bringing his face closer to hers. The space between them was nonexistent as their bodies connected. Sage had started to pull at her top, wanting to have her right there outside the club until a roar of a bike grabbed their attention. They pulled apart from each other as they faced the noise, noticing a pair of lights coming from a bike in the parking lot. They watched as a woman got off the bike, neither of them recognizing her face once her helmet is off.

"It must be the new woman," Mia whispered to Sage as their eyes followed her into the club. They tidied themselves up as they decide to follow her into the club. They needed to find out who she was and why she'd decided to come around.

They found her at the bar when they walked back into the club. No one dared make a sound as they all watched them approach her. Everyone in the club knew they needed to ask her questions. Everyone was dying to know who this new woman was, if she was part of the Omens they would have to get rid of her and fast. They couldn't have any trouble. Mia ordered a drink from

Mike, needing something to calm her nerves as she became aware of the role she now needed to play.

She knew it had taken a lot of guts to find Sage a few days ago and she was proud of how strong and powerful she had been. She knew that she would have to be that person again. She had to protect her new family. She wouldn't necessarily put a knife to the woman's throat as she had with the Omens but if she had to she would. She was the leader after all. She could even sense that Sage took her role seriously.

"You're not from around here," Mia stated as she sat down next to the woman. Sage didn't sit. Instead, he stood right behind Mia. She took a sip of the drink as she watched the woman shift in her seat. She clearly didn't like that Mia had claimed a spot next to her. Mia didn't waste any time. She didn't feel like there was any point in wasting time when there were questions that needed to be answered.

"Um, yes, I am," the woman replied, while she looked Mia up and down. Mia didn't like the way she looked at her, as if she were sizing her up for a fight. The last time that had happened to Mia she was almost strangled to death by an Omen. The thought sent a shiver down her spine. She had never fought a woman before. As a matter of fact, she had never fought anyone before and even when she had shown her power over the other two Omens, they had been tied up and basically helpless.

Mia hadn't learned how to fight so she knew she wouldn't be able to take anyone on if it came down to it. She may have been strong but she had no way of knowing how to fight another person.

"No one's seen you around, so I don't believe that," Mia said to the woman as she looked around the club to everyone while they watched the interaction between them. Mia knew that if anything they would all back her up if she needed it. She could count on them at least.

"Just because no one has seen me before doesn't mean I'm not from around here." Mia wasn't buying it. She couldn't have thought that was a good excuse. No one knew her and that was a fact.

"Uh huh." Mia took note of her attitude and she didn't like it. The woman seemed too sure of herself, too cocky for someone who didn't belong. Something wasn't right about her. She turned to Sage with a questioning expression on her face and he led her away. It was clear they wouldn't get very far with the new woman.

"What do you want to do?" he asked as they took a seat at a booth a little bit away from the unknown woman.

"I don't know," she said. She couldn't tell if the woman was a threat or not. They wouldn't be able to ignore her for too long.

They both sat and watched her for a while, trying to

pick up any hint that she could possibly be an Omen, but she didn't give anything away.

"I think we can leave her for now. She doesn't seem to be a threat," Mia said as she turned her head away from the woman to look at Sage.

"I agree," he replied with a small nod.

"I'll just tell the girls to keep an eye out for her when I'm not around."

"Good idea. We have to be on high alert from now on," he said.

They sat at the booth for a little while longer, watching the woman to see if she gave anything away, but she didn't. They decided to have a drink before they left just to calm down a bit as their nerves had peaked when the woman had arrived. Once they had both finished their drinks they headed home, calling a cab because they had both been drinking.

6

"Why do you love her?" Laura asked as we sat on a bench looking out at a lake.

"Why do you ask me such weird questions?" he asked with a laugh. His dreams with Laura had picked up but he was grateful because they were all pleasant dreams. She seemed to be at peace in his dreams and he hoped she was at peace.

"I'm just curious," she said. "You're not the type of person who just falls in love with just anyone."

Sage knew she was right, he didn't just fall in love with anyone. He had never been the type of man who wore his heart on his sleeve. He was protective of himself, more so after he had lost Laura.

"You do have a point there," he said. He wasn't sure if he wanted to answer her question though. He didn't feel comfortable telling his ex-partner why he loved someone new.

"You can tell me, you know. There's nothing I can do

*about it and we're at peace with each other now. Think of me as a friend," she laughed. It was hard to picture her as just a friend. After all, she was dead.*

*"Would it make you feel better if you knew why I loved her?" he asked.*

*"I wouldn't say that. She's just not like me, is she?" she asked. She was right. Laura and Mia were completely different people. They were both strong but personality-wise they were two different types of women.*

*"I don't know if you need to know why I love her. I don't want to hurt you," he said.*

*"You're not hurting me," she stated. It was unnerving just how persistent she was about it. Sage didn't see the point in sharing that with her, even if it was all in his subconscious.*

*"I don't want to share that stuff with you. Why can't we just sit here in each other's company?" he asked. He knew when his dream was over, he'd feel as if he really spoke to her and he thought it was his way of still having her near. She would always be a part of him.*

*"Okay, let's just sit in silence and watch the birds," she said. They faced the birds and watched as they flew higher and higher into the sky, disappearing into the light.*

Sage sat in his office and thought about the dream he had had the night before. The dream had again left him with a sense of peace when he had woken up. He and Laura were having a chance to talk and even if it wasn't real, he still believed it was a good sign.

His mind went to the new woman who had popped up in the area. He didn't like the unknown woman. When they had asked her who she was, she didn't give much information away which irritated him. Anyone would agree that when someone new arrives, everyone wants to know about them. That was just how it worked but this woman didn't want to give too much away and that didn't seem right to Sage. Why was she so hesitant to share who she was with people? What is she hiding, Sage thought. He was also extremely wary of new people, as was everyone else in the club. They were all tighter than ever now that Sage was back and no one would risk someone breaking that up.

She didn't come off as very smart either and the way she presented herself was peculiar. She talked without a filter, without an awareness that most people carried about themselves. He didn't know the woman but something about her didn't sit well with him. He had zoned in on his computer and hadn't paid attention to his surroundings until Mia waved her hand in front of his face, bringing him back to reality.

"Earth to Sage," she said as she saw his eyes focus on her hand. Mia remembered her dream from the other night as Sage stared vacantly into nothing. She couldn't imagine what he was thinking about but part of her hoped he could be thinking about her like he had been in her dream but she knew that was wishful thinking.

He smiled at her, gently batting her hand away as he focused on her. She was standing in front of him dressed in all black, looking sexy as hell and ready to kick some ass.

"I'm here," he said with a chuckle.

"I'm glad to hear it. I thought I had lost you there for a second," she replied with a laugh.

Sage brought his thoughts back to the present as he focused on some of the freckles across Mia's face. Man, she's beautiful, he thought as he almost got distracted by her face being so close to his.

"What can I do for you?" he asked. He knew she must've come to him for a reason. She had kept her distance whenever he went into the office. Not like when he had kicked her out before but out of respect, she didn't enter unless necessary.

"Well, I wanted to come in and share some news with you about the new chick," Mia said as she sat in the chair that was placed across from Sage and his desk. She made herself comfortable as she stared at him, wanting some sort of interest from him. It didn't take long for him to cave; his interest was peaked.

"What's the news?" he asked interested.

He hoped it was that she had already left and wasn't even a problem anymore but that would be wishful thinking. After all, she had only just shown up.

"It seems that one of the girls got their phone stolen

and although they can't prove it, they suspect it was this new woman," Mia said. It didn't make any sense. Why would she steal a Hell Kat's phone? It wasn't like they would have any valuable information on it.

"Why would she steal a phone?" Sage asked.

"Well, that's just it. We don't know why. None of the Hell Kats keep important information on them, that all stays here with us," Mia replied. Sage nodded in agreement. Everything was kept between them, no one knew much of anything.

"How can we be sure it's her?" Sage asked. It wasn't that he didn't believe the story. He just wanted to be sure that whatever move they made next was the right move for the club.

"There's no evidence that is was her but that's where the story takes a turn," she replied. Mia knew that the minute she told Sage about what had happened, he'd want the woman out and luckily Mia had her own plan when it came to that. She enjoyed who she was when it came to threatening people. It was weird but she felt so powerful and strong in those moments that she almost fed off the power she felt. It made her feel like a bigger version of herself and no one could say that was something bad. She knew Sage would also want a part in taking care of business but she knew it was something she had to do on her own. Woman to woman.

"What's the rest of the story?" Sage asked. The suspense was killing him.

"She tried to break into the office at the club, and when one of the Hell Kats caught her, she tried to hit on her as a distraction," she said.

The hitting on the Hell Kat part wasn't the problem but the fact that she was trying to break into the office was a big red flag. What could she be looking for, Sage wondered.

"We can't let this go any further. We literally just got out of some serious shit and this doesn't sound any better to me," he replied.

"I'm already on it. I'll be back once I've taken care of business," Mia replied with a cheeky grin.

"Are you sure you don't want me to come with? I can help," he said.

"I'll be fine, Sage, trust me. I've handled worse," she replied. Sage knew she was talking about the Omens. He had gotten more information about that and it was amazing to hear how strong Mia had been. She had placed herself in a situation and had shown she wasn't someone to mess with.

"Be careful," Sage called as Mia stood to leave.

"Don't worry about me, I'll be fine," she replied as she left the office.

The problem was that Sage would worry, he knew Mia was strong and at this point, she was capable of anything, things he hadn't seen yet. He had heard about what she did when she was interrogating the Omens so he knew she was feisty when necessary but since he hadn't exactly been able to tell her how he felt about her, he worried about anything that could bring her danger. He knew he wasn't ready to utter those three words yet but whenever Mia was apart from him he worried that, like in the well, maybe he wouldn't get the chance.

He thought about the woman who had just threatened the peace they had just gotten back and something in the back of his mind set off an alarm bell. There was something about her that seemed familiar, he just didn't know what. He knew he would have to do more research on her once he got her name. She hadn't told them when they had tried to ask her who she was which made her even stranger. It didn't make sense that someone would be that secretive about their identity unless they were hiding something and hiding something huge. Sage didn't like the idea of there being a new threat to him and Mia. He had to think about her more now because he wanted to protect her no matter what.

7

Mia made her way to the club. She couldn't let the woman's actions slide, not after all the trouble she had caused in such a short period of time. The club was busy when Mia arrived. She didn't bother to stop at the bar. Instead, she headed straight to the back office, only nodding her head as everyone greeted her on her way. She didn't have time for chit chat, not today. They all already know why she was there so no one bothered to stop her either. She looked like she was ready for business and she was.

She knew she would do anything to make sure the new woman would realize that she had come to the wrong place to mess with people. They didn't want her around and they would get rid of her. They had to get rid of her. The only people welcomed by the Screaming Demons were people Fiona and Grier told them about and this woman had come out of nowhere. It wasn't a good sign and Mia knew it.

Mia thought of all the possible reasons this new woman could be around. She didn't seem to know anyone because she was always by herself but what could she be looking for if she was trying to break into the Screaming Demons' offices, Mia wondered. They didn't really keep a lot of things in the office. Most of the information was kept at the house with Mia and Sage, which seemed like an excellent idea considering the possible break-in.

As she entered the office she could feel the tension coming from the girls, all of them waiting, ready to pounce if need be. There were three of them standing around the woman while she sat in the chair facing the desk. A sense of pride ran through Mia. She had the best team anyone could ask for.

"Well," she started as she made her way across the small office to take the seat behind the desk. "It looks like little miss nobody has been quite the trouble maker," she said matter of factly. The woman looked at her. She didn't appear to be intimidated by Mia at all.

"My name is Lorraine," she stated.

"I prefer miss nobody, that's what you are to me, nobody. You're just someone asking for attention, and the attention you're getting is not the attention you want," Mia warned. She needed to make sure the woman knew she wasn't wanted around the club or around them. They knew how to deal with trouble and Mia had no problem with sorting her out if she had too. She would fight if she had to. She still wouldn't know exactly what to do but she would stop at nothing to win.

"I'm not here to seek attention," Lorraine replied.

"Then why are you here and why are you trying to break into my office?" she asked. Lorraine looked at her sheepishly. Clearly, she hadn't wanted to get caught.

"I wasn't trying to break into your office," she said. Mia couldn't believe her lies. Surely she couldn't have thought she would get away with it.

"Oh, is that right? Please explain to me exactly what you were doing with my office door then, when you were caught on your knees with a bobby pin in the keyhole?" Mia asked with raised eyebrows. She was curious about what her excuse would be.

"Um, um, it's not what it looked like," she said. Mia almost laughed in Lorraine's face. There was no way she could think that was a good enough answer.

"Listen, if you leave now I won't bother calling the cops and getting you arrested for breaking and entering," Mia said. She didn't want to play any more games.

"But I didn't break into anything," she replied.

"You clearly have no idea who you're messing with." Mia knew she didn't have any Omen symbols on her so to her it would be easy getting rid of Lorraine. She had friends around that were involved with the cops, and they would help her out no problem.

"Please, I'm not here to cause any trouble," she begged, sensing the seriousness in Mia's voice.

"You see the problem there is that you've already caused trouble. We want you to leave," Mia demanded.

"I promise, I won't try anything again. I was just curious," she pleaded.

"Curious about what?" Mia asked.

"I was just curious as to what was in here."

Her excuses are pathetic, Mia thought to herself. No normal person would break into someone's office just out of curiosity's sake.

"It's too late for promises and excuses. You don't belong here so it's best that you leave now before you regret it," she said. The Hell Kats behind Lorraine had already made their way to the door. They lined up on either side of the open door as Mia stood up, reinforcing her demands. Lorraine looked around, pleading with her eyes as she looked at them all. They turned away from her, showing their loyalty to Mia. They all wanted her to leave and the sooner the better.

"Okay, I'll leave," she said as she got to her feet. She quietly walked out of the door, her shoulders straight but a look of hurt in her eyes. In a way, Mia related to her. She had held that look and walk so many times before when she had tried to keep a brave face but knew she was defeated. She didn't let her emotions stop her from doing the right thing though as she watched Lorraine leave. It's for the best, she thought.

It seemed too good to be true though. Why had she shown up if she was just going to leave so quickly, Mia thought, it didn't make any sense. She had tried to fight to stay and she had denied all the things she was accused of but she had still left without much of a fight. It couldn't be over just like that. There had to be more to it, there had to be more to who this woman was. Mia knew she would have to look her up when she got home. Lorraine was too strange just to stop in and leave like that and Mia suspected it was only the beginning.

Once she was out of the room the girls closed the door behind her. Mia slumped back into her chair. She knew she was the lead but it was tiring having to make sure nothing went wrong.

"We must keep our eyes and ears open for anything that could be a threat to us. If she has tried to break into the office, who knows what she already knows," Mia stated as she looked from each girl, all of them nodding in unison.

"What should we do if she comes back?" one asked. Mia thought about it for a while. She hoped she wouldn't try to come back but she knew what they'd have to do if she did.

"We have to kick her out if she comes back. We don't have room for troublemakers," she said.

"How should we kick her out?" The question hung in the air. Mia hadn't thought about it but she didn't want it to be a scene if the time came.

"Do it gently, I don't want there to be a scene. Do whatever you can to get her out. She can't be trusted," she replied. The girls knew she was right. She dismissed them and sat in her office for a while. The woman reminded her of someone, maybe herself, she couldn't put her finger on it but she was gone now and Mia could relax. She didn't see any point of staying at the club any longer so she decided to go home so she could be with Sage. Being around him would definitely make her calmer. She left the club, riding her bike instead of calling for a taxi.

She thought about the woman on her way home, how she had acted, and it didn't really make her feel safe. She had been so dismissive and so withdrawn it didn't make sense that she would have tried to break into an office. The whole situation didn't sit well with Mia.

8

As the house got closer into view, Mia's nerves calmed but peaked at the same time. The thought of Sage being so close made her excited. They had been getting on so well that Mia felt like they could soon be a proper couple, though neither of them brought the topic up. She would wait for Sage to say something to her about it, just to be sure she wasn't the only one thinking that way.

As she walked into the house she could smell food cooking away. The air was filled with different aromas, all of which tingled her taste buds. She usually cooked every night. She didn't mind so much since she enjoyed cooking but clearly Sage had different ideas for that night. The thought of him cooking for her made her think that there could be hope for them after all. She tried not to get her hopes up as she entered the house.

"Sage?" she called as she locked the door behind her. She wasn't so worried about anyone breaking into the house but she had become aware of security. She felt the need to look over her shoulders more than she ever had before, scared that someone could be lurking in the darkness, ready to take her or Sage. The thought haunted her.

"In the kitchen," he shouted back. She made her way to the kitchen and found Sage standing over a pot, stirring it vigorously. Steam came out of the pot and Mia noticed how high the temperature was as she walked closer to the stove. She had never seen Sage in the kitchen before besides him just joking with her while she cooked. She wanted to reach over and change the heat setting because it was way too high but she didn't want to interfere with his task.

"Welcome home," he beamed at her with a look of pride on his face. It was clear he had taken it upon himself to cook them dinner instead of waiting for Mia to arrive home. The thought meant a lot to her and so she couldn't help but smile when she looked at Sage. He looked gorgeous and her heart throbbed for him.

"What are you doing?" she asked. She had no idea exactly what he was cooking and by the look of his face neither did he. She looked into the pot and only saw a lot of brown liquid with chunks. It didn't exactly look pleasing to the eyes.

"Well, you've been taking such good care of me recently and I mean you did also save my life not so long ago that I thought maybe it would be nice for me to take care of you a little," he said with a shy smile. Mia's heart almost leaped out of her chest right then and there, wanting to escape her body and make a new home next to Sage's own heart. She had hardly ever been taken care of. She had always looked after herself and she took on the mommy role most of the time too so she would look after those around her. It was a nice change to feel looked after for once and she appreciated it.

"That's so sweet of you," she replied as she walked into the kitchen and gently touched his arm. "So what's for dinner?" she asked. As she looked further into the pot she still couldn't figure out what it was. There wasn't much color and it seemed to be going from brown to almost black.

"Well, it's a lamb stew. I thought it would be the easiest thing for an unprofessional cook to make. Turns out it isn't that easy," he said with a laugh. She chuckled slightly with him. She grabbed a spoon and dipped it into the pot so she could taste it, and to her surprise, it didn't taste bad at all.

"It just needs a bit more salt and maybe turn the heat down but other than that I think it's perfect," she said as she brushed her lips against his cheek, showing her gratitude. He smiled, sprinkled a little salt into the pot and tasted it himself. She could tell he was chuffed with himself.

"Well, chef Sage, while you finish up here I'm going to jump into the shower quickly. I feel like I need to get my last interaction off my skin," she said referring to her chat with Lorraine.

"Did it go alright?" he asked.

"As well as it could have," she replied while she walked in the direction of her bathroom. "I'll tell you all about it when I'm done," she said. Sage didn't say anything and instead focused on cooking.

Mia decided to have a bubble bath as she wanted to relax a bit after her chat. Her muscles had started to tense and with her gyming more frequently her body ached as a consequence. She ran a hot bath and filled it with one of her bath soaps. A calming scent of lavender filled the room and she already felt calmer. She took her time as she washed the day away, scrubbing her skin and feeling almost new again. Once she was done and dressed in fresh pajamas she joined Sage in the dining room which he had already set up. They both dug into the stew Sage had cooked. To the shock of both of them, it was actually delicious in the end.

"This is an amazing meal, Sage. You should be proud of yourself," Mia said as she watched Sage blush at the compliment.

"Thank you, that's so kind of you to say," he replied.

He hadn't cooked for anyone before so he was glad his efforts were taken so well. He thought he had almost messed the meal up. It was close to burning before Mia had turned up so he was pleased that it had actually turned out well.

"You should cook more often," Mia teased. She could tell he had been nervous when she had gone for the first fork full of stew but his shoulders relaxed once he knew he did a good job.

"Don't be cocky now, it may have been a once in a lifetime opportunity," he laughed. The atmosphere around them was light and soon the topic changed as they talked a bit about how the chat went with Lorraine. Mia told Sage they had gotten her to leave.

"I just hope she doesn't come back," she said.

"I'm sure she won't. She must know there is no place for her," Sage replied. He liked how stern Mia had been with the woman; it turned him on. When dinner was done and the place all tidied up, Sage took Mia by her hand and led her to his room. He wanted her desperately.

As they both lay panting, coming down from their ecstasy high, the conversation went back to Lorraine.

"Do you want to get out of the club?" Sage asked. Mia was a bit taken aback by his question but replied almost immediately.

"No, I don't. It's family to me and I don't want to lose

that," she replied. She knew the current problems within the Screaming Demons seemed to be picking up but she couldn't imagine herself anywhere else.

"Do you want to leave?" she asked Sage.

"No, I don't want to leave either. There's just a lot that concerns me," he replied.

"I know and I'm concerned too but Fiona and Grier won't let anything get too far."

"I know they won't but there are just too many threats and attention coming to the club. What if they can't cover it all up?" he asked.

Mia knew Sage had a point. With everything going on, there was only so much they could all do. She didn't want to leave nor did she want to lose her place in the club. She liked the person she had recently grown into and she had the Screaming Demons to thank for that. Her mind traveled to her paintings. She had been doing more of them in her free time and she had started to notice the light coming in. She knew some of it was because of Sage being home but she also knew it was because she felt at home and she hadn't had that feeling in a long time.

She remembered how she had felt when she left home, her parents' disapproval of her, their disappointment in her when she hadn't been the daughter they had wanted. She knew she didn't owe them anything but she did owe herself and finding a home where she could finally fulfill her dreams meant so much to her. She could never leave.

"I'll fight whatever comes our way, Sage. Whoever comes after the Screaming Demons comes after me too and I will take them down," she stated. "I'll never leave."

Sage looked at her. Hearing the seriousness in her voice he knew she meant what she said and he knew that wherever she was he would be there too. They fell asleep in each other's arms.

*"Come on, you're going too slow!" a little voice shouted. Mia turned and saw a little boy with a trolley close behind him. It appeared that the trolley was attached to a dog who was supposed to be pulling the trolley.*

*"What's the problem, handsome?" Mia asked. The boy looked up at her with tears in his eyes. He was close to letting them run down his cheeks before he sniffed and blinked them away.*

*"Dodger is going too slowly. He needs to run!" the boy explained. The dog that was pulling the trolley looked exhausted and extremely old.*

*"I think Dodger is tired," Mia tried to explain. The boy looked shocked at the idea.*

*"But we've just started playing, Mommy," he said to her. She reached over and ruffled his hair. His cute little voice ringing in her ears.*

*"I know you have but you see Dodger is getting old, sweet-*

*heart. He can't play for too long anymore," she said. The little boy looked at the dog, sadness crossing his face.*

*"Is he going to die?" he asked.*

*"Of course not!" Mia said as she tried to reassure the child.*

*"Hey! Let's go! We have places to be and people to see," Sage called from behind them. Mia smiled at her little family.*

Mia smiled and sighed in her sleep as she zoned in on the dream she was having, allowing it to fill her heart with happiness and love. She slid closer to Sage in her sleep, his body bringing a sort of reassurance to her as she inhaled his scent. Her dreams with Sage had increased the more she slept next to him, though she didn't mind that much. They brought her happiness because it made her look forward to sleep. Her dreams were the one thing she could have that no one could take away from her. They were a secret life that she could create where she and Sage were together and had a family.

## 9

The next day, Mia woke up next to Sage. His eyes flickered as he continued to sleep. He looked so peaceful, his hair a mess while he lay flat on his stomach, breathing heavily in his sleep. She lay there for a while taking him all in. She noticed his lips move softly as he talked a bit in his dreams. His voice was too low for her to hear what he was saying but she watched as he dreamed. Mia knew he was sleeping better. He hadn't been screaming in his sleep as he had before and a part of her thought it was because of her being there with him although she didn't want to get her hopes up. She knew at some point he'd probably still need help with what he had been through and although they hadn't spoken about therapy again, she couldn't help but think that he would still need it eventually. Mia was told that he hadn't gotten over what had happened when he was in Afghanistan. She couldn't imagine how he must have felt when he woke up realizing he was the only one who had survived and she also couldn't imagine what demons had come out while he was trapped in the well. She could see he had become happier though, more willing to talk to her, to be around her but she still didn't know what was underneath it all.

She couldn't believe how much their relationship had changed recently. The burning in her chest grew every day. She knew the words were bound to tumble out of her mouth soon and she felt it was a good time to say them, right then while Sage lay asleep and unaware.

"I love you," she whispered. Sage didn't move but continued to breathe, the blanket around him moving ever so slightly as his chest pulled against the bed and his back lifted with each exhale. Mia knew he hadn't heard her, and she was grateful. It felt good to let the words fall out into the air, filling her ears with certainty. She had never said those words to a man before and a part of her was thankful because she knew she had saved them for the right person. There were a lot of things that were new to her because of Sage that he wasn't aware of which made her connection to him even stronger from her side. She wasn't sure exactly how he felt about her in return but when she sometimes caught him looking at her she thought she could see the love in his eyes.

She snuck out of his bed and crept into the little art room she created. She felt the need to paint something that showed how happy she was. She reached for a blank canvas, and placing it before her, she reached for a paintbrush. She grabbed her first color, red. She painted and painted and painted, dipping her brush into different colors as she went. Allowing herself to lose control as she continued to let her hand do the work. She felt content and happy the more she worked. Sweat slightly crossed her forehead, but she didn't stop. Soon a heart was on the canvas with different shades of red and pink radiating from it. She took her time detailing it with veins, it was her heart and it was alive. She could see the difference in herself and in her paintings over the past few days. She didn't have much black in any of her paintings; they were all colorful and bright, much like her world.

Sage woke up surprised to find his bed empty. He loved waking up with Mia next to him. It brought him a sense of peace whenever he looked over and saw her little body next to his so he was disappointed to find she wasn't there. He rolled over onto her side of the bed, inhaling the scent of her skin and perfume that still lingered. He lay in his bed for a while, reliving the dream he had woken up from, wishing it were real.

*Mia stood before him, her left hand stretched out in front of her, reaching out to him.*

"Come on, Sage, let's go," she said.

"Where are we going?" he asked as he took her hand. He didn't care where they were going though; he would go anywhere with her. She looked like an angel, wearing all white with a huge amount of light surrounding her.

"You'll see," she said with a cheeky grin. He wanted to kiss her right then. She pulled him toward a door he hadn't noticed before, and they made their way out into the garden that was just outside. It was beautiful, filled with growing rose bushes and the greenest grass he had ever seen. There were a few weeping willows in one corner that covered half a pond which was covered in water lilies.

"It's so beautiful," he said as he turned to face Mia who had an enormous grin on her face.

"It is, isn't it?" she breathed as she too took some time to look around the garden. She then pulled him toward a bench that was beneath one of the weeping willows, pulling him down with her as she took a seat. He wrapped an arm around her shoulders as they sat in silence for a while.

"I love you," she said, her voice radiating through his body, sending a shiver down his spine.

"I love you too," he replied. They looked at each other with love and happiness in their eyes. They both then turned to look out at the garden before them, both of them radiating with light.

The dream felt extremely real to Sage, as if he had heard Mia actually tell him those three wonderful words. He hadn't said those words to another woman besides Laura and a part of him wished he could say them to Mia. He knew she deserved it and yet he wasn't ready for it yet. He knew it was just a dream though and so he decided he would have a shower to get it off his mind. Out of the shower and dressed in clean clothes, Sage felt the need to look for Mia. He wanted to see her since he hadn't when he had woken up.

Once he was done applying his cologne and ready to face the day, he went searching for Mia. He wanted her face to be the first thing he saw every morning. She was so beautiful when she woke up and it almost amazed him.

He had noticed how she had claimed the one empty office for herself and although Sage was curious, he never dared go into it. He would only do that if Mia invited him herself which she hadn't. He looked into her bedroom which he found was empty so he tried the office. It was locked and after knocking, Mia responded.

"I'll be out in a minute!" she shouted through the door.

Instead of disturbing her any further, Sage made his way to the kitchen for his morning cup of coffee. He still felt half asleep even after his hot shower. He sat at the kitchen table as he wondered what Mia could be doing in that room. Maybe she was working on her lap dance moves, he thought, although she was already pretty good at that. Images of her dancing in front of him filled his mind as his eyes glazed over and he went deeper into thought.

He continued to quietly think to himself, only stopping when he heard feet tapping against the floor coming toward him.

He smiled as he saw Mia come into view. She was still in her pajama bottoms while she had one of his shirts on, hanging loosely against her body. She looked extremely cute, he thought to himself, he would give her all of his shirts to wear since she looked so good.

"Good morning," he said, "can I make you some coffee?" She smiled and nodded her head.

"Yes, please," she replied. He walked over to the kettle, placed some coffee and two sugars in a mug before adding milk and the already boiled water. He already knew how she liked her coffee.

"Thank you," she said as she took the coffee into her hands. Mia hadn't realized just how much attention Sage had been paying to her as she watched him make her coffee. They sat quietly in each other's company, just enjoying being around each other. Once Mia had finished her coffee and placed the empty mug in the sink, she bent over and kissed Sage quickly.

"I'm going to go back to what I was doing," she said as she started to walk back to the office.

"Okay," he said, "have a good day."

"You too!" and then Sage was alone again. He could go and ask her if he could see what she was doing but decided against it as he had other business to attend to.

He placed his empty mug next to Mia's and made his way toward the door. As much as he'd love to spend another day wrapped up in a world of their own, he knew he had a job to do.

He got on his bike, relaxing against its body as he roared it to life, loving the feeling of it growling beneath him. He opened the gate and slowly pulled out of the garage, noticing a car just outside the gate. He recognized it. It had been there for a few days and something about it didn't feel right to Sage. He knew almost immediately someone was spying on him and Mia. He knew it was the only possible reason why a car would continue to stay parked outside the house. He couldn't keep this information from Fiona and Grier so before he got out of the gate he pulled his phone out, dialing Grier's number as he took off his helmet to place the phone to his ear.

It didn't take long at all for Grier to pick up the call.

"Hi, Grier," he said into the phone.

"Sage, how are you feeling?" Grier asked. Although Sage wanted to get straight to the point of the phone call, he also didn't want to be rude to his boss.

"I'm doing well, thank you. Pretty much back to my old self," he replied and it was true. With the help of

Mia, he hadn't had to deal with any traumatic dreams like he had in the past.

"That's fantastic to hear!" Grier said, clearly thinking the call was just for a casual conversation. Sage knew that was about to change pretty soon though.

"So the reason I called was…" he started to say but got interrupted by Grier's voice.

"Sounds like there's a problem."

"There might be a slight problem," Sage replied.

"Well, what is it?" Grier demanded.

"I've noticed a car parked outside the driveway recently," Sage replied.

A moment of silence.

"How many times have you seen it?" It was no longer Grier's voice. Instead, it was Fiona's. Clearly, Grier had put the call on loudspeaker so they could all chat together.

"Oh, hi, Fiona. Um, I'd say three days, maybe four," he replied. He wasn't sure who it could be but he knew whoever it was, they were there for a reason.

"This doesn't sound good," Fiona said. Sage agreed.

"What should I do?" he asked. He already knew what he had to do but before he did anything he wanted to make sure they were all on the same page.

"Firstly stay indoors for a while, at least until we have some information as to what could be going on and secondly see if you can get any details on the car and send it our way. That would help," Grier said as he took over the conversation from Fiona.

Sage hoped they wouldn't have to stay indoors for too long. He hadn't realized how much he had missed riding until he had started his bike just moments ago.

"No problem, I'll do that. I'll have a look as soon as possible," he replied.

"Perfect. Sage, we know you've got it covered until we have definite answers, but stay out of trouble, won't you?" Grier said with a slight chuckle. Sage smiled. He would gladly follow those orders.

"Absolutely, Grier!" he said.

"Perfect. Contact us when you have information!" Grier said before hanging up the phone. Sage would happily go up to the car and beat whoever was in it to a pulp but he knew better. Instead, he reversed back into the driveway and closed the gate again. He would have to tell Mia about the car and make a plan from there.

He placed the bike back into the garage before he headed back into the house. He was grateful to find Mia sitting in the kitchen eating breakfast. It meant he wouldn't have to knock on the locked door again.

Mia looked at him with a surprised expression. She clearly hadn't expected him to be back so soon. After all, he had only been a few minutes.

"I thought I heard you pull out of the driveway?" she

asked, the question not really directed at him but to herself.

"I was pulling out of the driveway until I noticed a strange car just outside the gate. I've seen it there for a while and after speaking to Fiona and Grier about it, they think it's best that we stay inside until we know what we're dealing with," Sage replied as he joined her at the kitchen table. He could see concern cross her face as she took the information in.

"Who do you think it could be?" she asked. Sage had a few ideas but wasn't exactly sure.

"If I had to guess, I would say either we have an Omens problem again or it's law enforcement," he stated. He didn't want to scare her but he had learned that she was tougher than she looked and a lot tougher than he had thought when he had met her.

"This isn't good at all," Mia said as she shook her head. If it were the Omens, Sage knew they could take care of it like they had in the past but if it was law enforcement, there wasn't much they could do.

"We're a bit screwed if it's law enforcement," Mia said as if she was reading his mind.

"Yes, unfortunately. But we don't know who they are so there's no point in getting worried just yet," he said as he reached for one of the hands that she had placed on either side of her plate, forgetting her half-eaten breakfast.

"Yes, you're right. Let's not worry just yet," she smiled at him and although he could tell she was keeping her cool he could sense a lot of thoughts going through her head.

"We'll face whatever comes our way, together."

age and Mia spent the day indoors as they had been ordered. They didn't exactly spend the whole time together but they were aware of each other as they went about their day, finding things to do to fill their time. They had been spending so much time together that it didn't bother them too much if they were apart for a while. They loved each other's company but sometimes things didn't have to be done with the other there.

Mia took it upon herself to do some cleaning. She hadn't done much cleaning since Sage had come home. Her attention seemed to gravitate to him most of the time and so she was shocked when she noticed how much mess there was. She went into every room so she could move furniture, sweep the floors, mop, dust and then place everything back the way it was. She wanted the house to be spotless like it should've been before her cleaning spree. She went from room to room, taking her time so she could keep herself busy. She enjoyed cleaning so she didn't mind the task she had taken. Once she had completed that, it was lunchtime and so she decided to make lunch for both herself and Sage who had taken the other office so he could do some work from home.

"Knock, knock," she said as she walked into the office. Sage looked at her with surprise. He had been absorbed by whatever work he had been doing before she arrived.

"Hey," he said as she stood before him. He looked like a proper businessman as his face was zoned in on his computer.

"I was thinking of making some lunch. Would you like some?" she asked. She was tired from all the cleaning and could do with a break and something to eat.

"Oh, that would be great. The time has completely slipped my mind." He chuckled as he noticed it was already 1 pm.

"Time slips by when you're having fun," she laughed mockingly. The time had seemed to drag for Mia while she had been cleaning. She normally enjoyed cleaning but with the law enforcement officers outside and the new woman making an appearance so close together, her mind had been running while she worked.

"You're definitely right," he laughed. He didn't seem like he was having fun as Mia noticed a few worry lines on his forehead. Clearly, he had been thinking about their situation too.

"Is there anything in particular you'd like to eat?" she asked. Getting a request would be easier but she knew cooking for Sage would be easy. He ate just about anything placed in front of him.

"Surprise me!" he replied.

"A surprise coming right up! Feel free to join me in the kitchen when you're done!" she said as she headed to the kitchen herself.

What can I make for lunch, she asked herself. She knew she would still probably have to cook dinner in a few hours so she didn't want to make anything too heavy for lunch. She decided on ham, cheese and tomato sandwiches, and she'd toast them too.

Luckily she had done some shopping a few days before so the fridge was packed and had the ingredients she needed.

She took out a chopping board and sliced the cheese and the tomato into thick enough slices. Placing a pan on the stove, she started to heat up some butter as she layered the ingredients in the bread. She also added a thin layer of mayonnaise to the bread. As she placed the first sandwich into the pan, Sage popped his head around the corner.

"I love the smell of melting butter," he said as he sniffed the air. "Can I help with anything?" he asked.

"I've got everything under control," she replied as she flipped the first sandwich, revealing a delicious golden brown toasted slice of bread.

"That looks fantastic," he said.

"It does, doesn't it?" she said with a proud smile.

Sage looked at her as she stood in the kitchen, claiming the area around her. She looked happy and radiant, she almost took his breath away. He'd caught himself staring at her when she wasn't looking, admiring her from afar. He could get used to the idea of her in the kitchen of a house they could call their own. Something about the way she moved, picked this up and placed that there, kept his attention every time and he knew it made the feelings he had for her grow inside, almost uncontrollably. He enjoyed it though. As difficult as it had been to admit his feelings to himself, she had made falling in love feel easy, and it felt amazing. He had never had this much of a wonderful experience with love before, even when it came to Laura which he knew would always be his first love but she had been so different from him, so unaware of him and his needs and though it had worked for a while his feelings for Mia were different, more complete. She had proved herself to him time and time again, making it impossible for him to push her away and he never wanted to push her away again, not when life looked so good with her in it.

Mia felt Sage's eyes boring into her back as she toasted the final sandwich and she smiled to herself.

"Why don't you set the table?" she asked, breaking him from his trance.

"Yes, of course. I'm happy to help," he replied as he grabbed plates and placed them on the table with two glasses. There wasn't any need for knives and forks. "Shall I put out some juice?" he asked.

"That's a great idea. Pick a flavor from the fridge," she replied.

He opened the fridge and pulled out orange juice and soon they were both sitting at the table eating lunch.

"I can't remember the last time I had a toasted sand-wich," he said as he bit into his sandwich. "It's like child-hood in flavors," he finished.

"I agree. My mom used to make me sandwiches after school and I lived for them. Even as simple as they are, they're just so good," she said. They sat in silence as they devoured their lunch, both thinking of their childhood, remembering the simpler days as kids. After they had finished lunch and had a glass each of orange juice everything was cleaned and packed away, leaving no dirt in sight. Mia is serious about cleanliness, Sage thought to himself, making a note to try not to be a messy person. He knew that would be hard though.

Sage went back to his office while Mia started doing loads of laundry, the pile of clothes from both of them had started to get a bit too much for her to handle. She was quietly humming to herself as she worked, feeling at peace as she separated clothes, placed them in the washing machine and hung them up to dry once they were done. She was slightly exhausted by the time she had finished ironing all the clean clothes and once she had placed them all back into their cupboards, she decided to take a shower. She felt a bit sweaty from her day of cleaning and washing, even though she had loved every second of it. She was satisfied with her work for the day. She stepped into the shower and washed herself thoroughly, washing the day away which felt extremely long now that she had stopped distracting herself from the possible threat outside her house. She hoped the car parked outside belonged to the Omens because she knew then it wouldn't be too much of an issue. They had dealt with worse than a parked car and they could take care of them but if it was law enforcement she had no idea what would happen then.

"Mia, I'm just stepping out quickly. I won't be long!"

Sage called from outside her bathroom door. She couldn't imagine where he would be going now but she didn't question him.

"Alright!" she replied.

Mia was more terrified of Sage leaving the house the longer he was gone. She didn't understand why he would go out if he had just told her that they were not to leave the house. Was he trying to leave without telling her, she thought. That wouldn't make any sense though considering they had gotten closer recently. Maybe they had gotten too close, maybe Sage didn't want her anymore. That thought terrified her even more. She still wasn't sure what they were. They did spend a lot more time together and she felt as if they were building some sort of relationship. The thought made her smile as she got out of the shower, trying her hardest not to think of the worst. She decided to start dinner while Sage was out. She didn't see the point in waiting for him to get back before she started. His appetite had increased since he had regained his strength so Mia cooked a lot to make sure he was always fed.

Sage decided that while there were still a few hours of daylight left it would be a good idea to check out the car more closely so he could send information back to Fiona and Grier.

He went back to his bike, started it up and opened

the gate in front of him and made it seem as if he was going out. He passed the car which hadn't moved since he had seen it in the morning and parked a little way away, out of their view. He got off his bike and walked closer, keeping out of sight so he could take the details of the number plate down on his phone and send it to Fiona. He watched as two large men got out of the car and walked over to the house. They definitely looked like law enforcement officers, Sage thought as he noticed their Oxford shirts. They walked over to the gate, although they didn't make any moves to try to break into the house. Even for them, that wouldn't be okay. They walked along the gate talking to each other as they looked at the house. It appeared as if they were discussing something but Sage couldn't be sure from his distance. He couldn't hear what they were saying. It didn't look good for them and Sage knew that. Someone had snitched on them or leaked something to the officers. They looked very interested in the house that Sage had just left. He didn't feel good about having left Mia there by herself so after waiting a good fifteen minutes he climbed back onto his bike and roared it back to life once more, and as he got closer to the house he saw the men run around a corner so they wouldn't be seen by him although it was too late. Sage already knew who they were.

He opened the gate and closed it quickly behind him. He didn't know why they were there and he didn't want to risk them being able to get into the house. As soon as he switched off his bike, his phone went off in his pocket. He looked at the name on the screen and saw it was Fiona calling. He answered as quickly as he could.

"Fiona," he said as he picked up the call, "what can you tell me?"

"Well, we're not sure why they're there but it's not looking good for us, Sage. They appear to be law enforcement officials." Sage nodded to himself, pleased he had managed to figure that out on his own.

"What do you need me to do?" he asked.

"You need to pack up and head back to Pine Hill. Both of you," Fiona said as she included Mia. Sage already knew he wouldn't leave without her either way but he knew she wouldn't be happy with leaving Florida.

"Yes, of course," he replied.

"We don't know all the details yet but I suggest you get out of there as soon as you can. We suspect that with you both showing up out of nowhere and the Omen ringleaders disappearing has brought a bit more attention to us than needed," she explained. It made sense to Sage. It was only since he and Mia had arrived that things started to change rather quickly, and now it seemed it was too quick.

"That makes sense," he replied.

"I'm glad we're on the same page, Sage. Now get your asses out of there," she said as the phone went silent.

Sage sighed to himself. He now had to break the news to Mia. This won't go down well, he thought as he walked back into the house.

"Mia?" he called out.

"Yes?" she shouted back. Her voice coming from the kitchen.

"I have some bad news," Sage said as he walked into the kitchen to find her sorting out food for dinner.

She stopped what she was doing as she looked over at him. She paid attention to his face, but he didn't give anything away.

"Well, what is it?" she demanded as she looked at him.

"We need to leave," he stated.

"Leave where?" she asked. In her heart, she knew the answer but she wanted to hear him say it.

"We need to leave Florida and head back to Pine Hill," he said with a grim smile. Her heart sank in her chest. She didn't want to leave.

"Do we have to?" she pleaded.

"Yes, Fiona's orders," he replied. He could see the look of upset in her eyes. "We don't have a choice."

"Who are they? The men?" she asked.

"They're law enforcement officials. We can't fight them," he replied.

"Shit, it's bad then, isn't it?" she asked.

"We don't know how bad but the fact that they're parked outside our house doesn't seem so good," he said. The mention of their house sent a feeling into Mia's chest. They would have to leave their house and they had just made it their own. The thought saddened her.

## 11

The more Mia thought about it, the sadder she got. All her life she had felt out of place, like she didn't truly belong anywhere and now she did. She belonged in Florida with the Screaming Demons and the Hell Kats. She had made herself into a person she loved and who people loved. She had made friends with everyone in the club, she had earned her place there and now she would have to leave because someone snitched on them.

"Is there nothing else we can do?" she asked. She knew what he'd say before he said it but she still didn't want the decision to be final.

"I'm sorry, Mia, but no, we have to leave," he replied. "If we stay here any longer, who knows what could happen. We could go to prison, for example."

Mia knew leaving was the only option they had but

she had just gotten comfortable in Florida and she had nothing in Pine Hill. She was just getting control of her life. She had the Hell Kats who she could always count on. They had all been there for her on the sidelines when Sage had gone missing, they would constantly check in on her, making sure she was okay. She loved them for it. She had also just been made a Screaming Demon and she wasn't sure how her role would change when they got back to Pine Hill. She had a family in Florida which made it harder for her to leave. She felt as if she had found a place where she belonged. She didn't have a family of her own, she didn't even know where her parents were and so the club was all she had.

"When do we have to leave?" she asked.

"Right now," he replied. Sage could see the sadness in Mia's eyes. He stepped toward her and took her face in his hands. He kissed her passionately for a while. He knew how much it all meant to her and he hated that they had been blind to the law enforcement officers in the first place. He knew they must've been watching them for a while but they had both been so caught up in their own little world that they didn't even notice the car parked outside.

"We'll come back, I promise," he said when he pulled away from her. Mia believed him. She knew that he would not only protect her but kept her best interests at heart.

"I guess I should go pack," she said as her lips tingled from the kiss. She almost had the urge to have Sage right there in the kitchen but she stopped herself. They didn't have time to stop and have sex, she thought, they had to catch a flight back soon.

They both headed back to their bedrooms to pack a few essentials, leaving most of their things behind in the hopes that they'd be back relatively soon.

They met at the door with carry bags in their hands.

"Well, I guess it's goodbye for now," Mia said as she looked around the house.

"We'll be back so yes, it's only goodbye for now," he said.

They called a cab and made their way to the airport where they boarded a plane to Boston.

Mia watched out the window of the plane as Florida went out of sight. Sage took her hand from next to her.

"I know it feels like home to you and I know it's important so we will come back as soon as the heat goes away," he said with a gentle squeeze of her hand.

Once the flight was over and they landed in Boston they made their way to meet Fiona and Grier. They would need a rundown of what to expect while they were back. They also needed to know exactly what was going on in the first place.

"Hi, guys. Thanks for coming back so quickly. Right now it's for the best," Fiona said.

Mia tried to put on a brave face as she nodded in agreement with Fiona. She understood that they couldn't risk being in Florida if law enforcement were on their trail but she already missed home. She longed to be in the kitchen cooking dinner and singing to the radio like she had been just not so long ago.

"If it's for the best, it's the only choice we have," Sage replied. Mia knew he was right, they were both right, but she wished she could have been in her home, the home she had made with Sage. She wondered if Sage would treat her differently now that they weren't in Florida, away from everyone.

"We're working on getting the heat off of us and the organization. It may take some time but it's the best we can do."

It was obvious that Mia was saddened by the news as Fiona reached out for her and took her to the side.

"I know you didn't want to leave, Mia, and to be honest I wish you didn't have to. I've seen how well you have been down there, what you've been doing for the club and I'm really proud but unfortunately, this is out of our control right now," Fiona said. She knew she was right, it wouldn't help anyone if they got caught up in something in Florida they couldn't get out of.

"You're right, I know you are. It's just hard to leave something I've worked so hard for."

"Once everything is cleared up, I'll need you and

Sage to go back. We're just in the process of shutting down some business with the Omens, mostly guns, but I have a feeling once that is sorted you'll be able to go back," Fiona said.

"I understand and I'll do whatever I can here to help with that," Mia replied.

Sage and Mia were given a place to stay for the meantime. It was a two-bedroom apartment. Fiona and Grier still wanted them to stick together even while they were away from their home. It wasn't obvious to them that they had gotten closer over the past few weeks. Sage didn't want it to be a known thing yet and he had explained that to Mia before they left.

*"I think it would be best if we didn't make anyone question what's going on between us," he said. Mia knew what he meant. He didn't want anyone to know about their relationship, although Mia wasn't even sure what they were herself.*

*"That's no problem, I understand," she replied. She didn't want to push the topic because she didn't want to hear anything she wouldn't like. She didn't know what Sage thought was going on, and she didn't want to know if they were just sleeping together and that was it. She wouldn't like it if it were just that so she was too scared to ask.*

"So, what now?" Mia asked Sage as they got to the little apartment they'd be staying in.

"Well, we have to wait it out, don't we?" he replied.

"I guess so but I'm not sitting on my ass doing nothing," she said.

Sage loved her attitude.

"Neither am I," he replied. He already had some ideas of his own.

## 12

Sage knew he couldn't just sit back and allow Fiona and Grier to do all the work so he decided to get some help from a private investigator to help get some heat off of them back in Florida. He knew he had to get back as soon as possible. Being away from Florida just didn't feel right after everything that had happened. As much as Mia saw Florida as her home, Sage felt the same. He didn't like being away from his house and the friends he had made.

He found it amazing how he had made new friends so unexpectedly. He didn't realize that his presence was liked so much in Florida. Obviously, he had tried to be someone they could talk to and he had always tried to make a friendship with his team so it wouldn't always be just work but when he had gone missing, he truly realized what he meant to everyone. They had all sent him messages, and some had called him to check-in. He was blown away by the support. He was grateful for them all.

He wasn't sure what he was looking for, but anything would help. He just wished he could be investigating himself. He preferred to do things himself so he could have more control over the situation and the speed of things. He knew it wasn't his job, but he also couldn't handle the fact that he couldn't be more involved. He felt sort of helpless as he waited for anything he could pass along to Fiona and Grier. He felt bad that he had not suspected something sooner, he felt like he had let them down, and although they hadn't said anything, he knew they must've felt it. He wanted to make it up to them any way he could.

It didn't take long for the investigator to come back with something that could do the trick. The investigator had managed to collect all the information they would need to get the law enforcement off their backs.

"I need to go see Fiona," he said as he entered the lounge. Mia looked up from the TV. She had been looking for something to watch while she had nothing to do. Sage could see how hard it was on Mia to come back and he knew it wasn't just because Florida was their home now. He wasn't just trying to get back to Florida for himself but also for Mia.

He knew it was because this place just held a lot of bad luck for her and a lot of bad memories he knew she would much rather forget but Sage knew that the past never truly stays there and sometimes it comes back to haunt people when they least expect it.

His memories of being in the army would always be with him no matter what he did. It had been hard to deal with for a long time, but Sage had sadly gotten used to the unexpected memories of his past. He obviously wished he could forget it all. He wouldn't have minded having his brain wiped of all of his past. His past didn't seem to matter so much with Mia around.

It was just the night before when he had a haunting dream again. If anything he wished the dreams would stop. It would make life a lot easier for him.

*Sage knew he was dreaming when he saw blood on his hands. He knew he hadn't gotten actual blood on his hands in his life, but he knew what it meant.*

*He tried to wipe his hands on his pants, wishing his hands were clean.*

*"No matter how hard you wipe your hands they won't be clean, Sage. It's all in your head," a voice said from behind him. He had thought his last interaction with Laura was when he had let her go, but that was not the case.*

*"What are you doing here?" he asked her as he looked at her.*

*She was clean, dressed in her army uniform with no injuries and no visible wounds. She looked as if she hadn't even been in the army but was more so dressed up in a costume for Halloween. It didn't look right to Sage. A part of him knew that he would picture Laura in her uniform for the rest of his life. It had, after all, been the last image he had seen of her. He didn't like the fact that she hadn't been given the chance to live her life the way she had pictured. He remembered how often she would talk about what she wanted to do when they got out of the army. She had told him she wanted to go to veterinary college. She knew she may have been the oldest student there, but she didn't care.*

*"Well, I could ask you the same thing. Why are you here?" she asked. She looked at herself in surprise as she took in her outfit. She also didn't understand why they were there.*

*Sage looked around him, unable to make out the setting until his eyes widened with recognition.*

*"This is the house I pictured for us," he said as he walked around an empty lounge area. He had thought a lot about where he would live with Laura when they would finally be free of the military. He had pictured a big house with enough room for children and a few animals; dogs mostly but possibly a cat for Laura. The empty house clearly showed that it just wasn't meant to happen.*

*"The house is empty, Sage. I can't be there to fill it with memories anymore. You know I'm gone," Laura said, "I told you that it's okay to let me go." He knew that she wouldn't hold it against him if he did move on. The subconscious Laura he saw had no problems with moving on with his life.*

*"I know you did, but I'll carry the guilt with me for the rest of my life," he replied.*

*"Sage, there was nothing you could do. You can't bring me back. You couldn't have stopped that bomb either," she said.*

*"I know, I know, but you don't know what it's like being the only survivor," he said in return. On a subconscious level, he thought he was going a little insane with how real the conversation felt.*

*"You earned it, Sage," she replied.*

*He wanted to believe her, but he still felt that his life had been meaningless.*

*He knew he needed to do something, something great, and something worth the second chance he had been given. Knowing that he had been given a second chance for a reason would be the one thing that could make Sage achieve something. He didn't have to prove he was worthy of the chance, but he had to make it mean something.*

The thought of his dream consumed him. He wished he could believe that he had been given a second chance for a reason, but he couldn't see it. He couldn't understand what that reason could be considering his life still hadn't amounted to much after all this time. If he thought about it, the only good thing he had going in his life was Mia.

Sage hadn't realized that he had zoned out until he heard Mia's voice.

"Shall I come with you?" she asked him with concern in her voice.

She must have noticed his minor lack of focus when his mind had drifted. He couldn't tell her what he was thinking about; he hadn't told anyone about his dreams before.

"I think it's best if you stay here," he replied. He knew that if she went with him, she would get her hopes up and he didn't want to be the one to burst that bubble in case they couldn't go back yet.

"Oh, okay, let me know what happens then," she said. He already saw the disappointment on her face, and she didn't even know about the information he had. He hadn't told Mia that he had hired a private investigator. He thought that it would be better that way in case he had nothing to show for his efforts.

"I won't be long," he replied as he headed out. He heard her yell in response but couldn't make out what she said as he closed the front door behind him.

Sage had nothing in this town. He had sold his apartment when he left for Florida. He didn't have any intentions of ever coming back; he didn't even have his bike which he longed for. He wouldn't have minded getting a little fresh air so he could get his mind straight. He had been thinking about Mia and just how much she had started to mean to him, but he also couldn't let his mind focus on that while there were bigger issues at hand.

Only once they were back in Florida would he let himself think about how much he wanted to be with Mia. It was too much of a distraction and he had to focus on getting them back there. He still hadn't admitted to himself how much she meant to him and he really wasn't ready to even think about it too much.

He called for a cab and made his way to the club. He had already called Grier to check where he could find Fiona. He would've preferred going to Fiona's house rather than the club. He hadn't been there since he had been taken from just outside the front doors, but he knew Fiona would be in the office there. The office where he had also had sex with Mia for the first time. This town held so many memories for Sage, both good and bad. He couldn't deny that being physical with Mia was exciting, and the passion that flowed between them couldn't be ignored either.

He arrived at the club and stood outside for a while just so he could compose himself. His head and knees ached with the memory of getting hit over the head and behind the knees. His mind gravitated back to the well. He would never be able to let those memories go. He knew they weren't as bad as what he had been through before, but it was yet another traumatic experience for him to go through. Although the Omens hadn't done much to him physically, the scars of the event were burned into his mind. He would always remember the darkness and the loneliness of those two days he was trapped, constantly wishing for death. He hated the fact that he had gotten that low. He had never really wished for death before that, and he felt as if he had been weak for thinking of it at that time.

It's okay, you've got this, he told himself. He couldn't let his memories overtake the mission he had at hand. The sooner he told Fiona about what he had, the sooner he could be out of Pine Hill. That was the only goal he had in mind. The moment he could leave, he could also leave all of his bad memories behind, hopefully once and for all.

He walked into the club and headed straight for the office. He had a stack of files in his hands that he had printed with all the information he needed to give to Fiona. It felt heavy in his hands due to the amount of hope he had in them. He silently clung to the hope and willed it to be what he needed to get out of shit creek.

Let this be our ticket out of here, he thought. He would do anything to go back to the place he called home.

He knocked on the door and waited for permission to enter. His heart had picked up in his chest, threatening to land on the floor in front of him.

"Come in!" Fiona yelled from the other side. Sage opened the door and walked into her office. Fiona was sitting behind her desk, staring at her computer. She looked up as Sage entered the room.

"Ah, Sage, what can I do for you?" she asked. She indicated for him to sit across from her, which he did.

"Well, actually it's more about what I can do for you," he replied. Without wasting any time he handed over the files he had in his hands. "I think you'll like what I've got."

Fiona raised her eyebrows, intrigued by what he had said. She glanced at the files, and her eyes widened as she read more carefully some of the information that was on them.

"Wow, Sage. This is wonderful, this is what we need to get the feds off our backs," she breathed as she continued to look the files over. Sage smiled to himself as he knew he had gotten what was needed to help with the heat back in Florida.

"Do you think this will be enough to allow us to go back to Florida?" he asked.

"I think it'll be more than enough. There's enough dirt here that anyone who messes with us should be scared," she replied. Sage had looked at the files before he had arrived, so he knew exactly what she was talking about.

Sage was extremely happy to have gotten that kind of answer from Fiona. He already knew that the files would be what they needed, but he had also tried not to get his hopes up. Anything could've happened, and after all, Fiona could've already had the information he had, and it could've still not been enough.

"Sage, are you still comfortable with what we do? This isn't exactly what you're used to considering it's nothing like the army," she said.

He was a little taken aback by her question. He hadn't expected her to ask him something like that. He knew that being in the army was nothing that he had expected, although who could really know what to expect when movies had been played out so dramatically, and the news had so much propaganda. The army hadn't made him a better person, and he knew that there were things that had happened that could never be undone, but he also wasn't as naive as he was when he joined. He was a different person back then, and he was a different person every day that had passed since. He knew he was stronger in some ways and weaker in others, but if anything, he had joined the army with an open mind.

Fiona and Grier felt like a family to him. He felt like no matter what he did, he'd always have people who cared for him and who would also do anything for him whereas when he had been in the army, it had been every man for himself.

He knew he had his team to rely on or to talk to while he was out in the field, but when it came to crunch time it didn't matter how close you were to someone, they would look after themselves before they would help anyone.

"I am comfortable. I know how things work, and I know the value of life. I'd do anything it takes to protect those I care about," he replied. He knew he had given the right answer, the answer Fiona had wanted to hear when she had asked the question. She nodded her head in agreement. He felt like maybe it could've been a test. Fiona had known he was in the army when she had hired him, she knew he had been exposed to a different life.

"I'm happy to hear that. We will always look out for you, no matter where you are, so never forget that. Now you can go back to Mia and tell her the good news. You two can go home," Fiona said with a smile.

Sage couldn't wait to tell Mia. He knew that she would be extremely happy with the news.

He thanked Fiona for her time and left. He wanted to get back to Mia so they could finally make their way home. The thought of calling Florida home and a home with Mia there made Sage that much more excited to see her. He couldn't wait to see the excitement on her face.

He called a cab and went to Mia. The excitement in his chest grew as he got closer to their temporary place.

He walked into the house and found Mia curled up

on the couch watching a movie. It seemed like a romantic comedy. Clearly she had tried to choose something to lift her spirits up. She looked so sad as she watched the movie, hardly even reacting to anything that happened on the TV.

"I have great news," he said as he walked into the room without fully announcing himself.

Mia looked up from the TV, half shocked to see him. She hadn't heard him enter. He made his way to the couch and sat next to her.

"Oh, you're back," she replied. Not taking in what he had said. She looked half dazed.

"Yes, I am back. And I have great news," he said again, making sure she heard him.

"I heard you the first time… what's that?" she asked. Her interest building.

"Well, pack your bags, we're going home," he replied with a huge grin.

Mia's mouth popped open as she stared at him with wide eyes, completely shocked, and taken aback. Sage wanted to laugh at her reaction, it was even better than what he had pictured.

"Are you serious?" she asked as she got off the couch.

Sage nodded his head. "Yes, I'm dead serious. Fiona has given us the green light to go back to Florida," he replied.

He could see the excitement in Mia's eyes as she took

it all in. Within a few seconds, she jumped on the couch and started bouncing on it, completely ecstatic.

"That is the best news I've heard all day," she shouted as she continued to jump on the couch.

"Haha, now get off there and pack!" Sage said as he headed for the room so he could start packing himself.

Mia soon joined him and started packing up her things. He could tell she wanted to be out of there as quickly as possible. They both did.

Going back to Florida had been all that Mia had thought about while they had been away. She had hardly eaten or managed to do much while they had been there. Fiona had given her strict instructions to wait it out and just be patient while she worked things out. She was the most patient person at most times, but she wanted to get involved. When Sage had gone out mysteriously she hoped it was because he knew something she didn't, and as much as she tried not to get her hopes up she wished silently that he could come home with good news so when he finally came home and told her they could pack their things and go she was completely over the moon. She hadn't been sure when Fiona would give them the go-ahead to go back. It could've been months, and she was thrilled it had only been a few days. It was her home, and she didn't want to leave it ever again.

She didn't know what they had found for Fiona to have given them the green light and as much as she wanted to know she decided not to ask. The Screaming Demons knew what they were doing and she trusted Fiona had given them the green light because they had cleaned up the mess the law enforcement caused. Mia hoped they were gone for good. It was almost terrifying thinking that people had been watching them as they had gone about their lives without even being aware of it at all. She shivered every time she thought about it.

"Let's go home," Sage said when they boarded their plane. Mia couldn't help but smile as he called it home. She was extremely overwhelmed with happiness at the thought of her and Sage being together. It felt like it could be possible after all. The fact that Sage had called it home meant something to Mia. It meant that he considered her to be family to him. In what way she wasn't sure but she didn't think about it too much. She was just excited to get back to where they belonged.

She boarded the plane with much impatience, her body constantly bouncing up and down as they flew across the sky. She tried to distract herself by looking out of the window and taking in the scene outside. She watched as the city became further and further away from her view. The excitement peaked inside her chest as Boston was almost out of view. It wouldn't be long until she could walk into her house again. She knew she would want to make it look more homely at some point. She thought about adding paintings around the house, not her own but something she and Sage would like. She made a list in her head of all the things she could do if it was going to be their home. She wanted it to look more like a home than a place where two people just lived.

Once they had landed and arrived back at the house, Mia went through every room, taking it all in. She hadn't been away from it for that long, but it definitely made her heart happy being there. She wanted to run around the entire house, but she held herself back. Instead, she breathed in with a flush of happiness that she felt so strongly since she had moved to Florida. She was relieved and extremely happy to be home. Pine Hill was the place of her past and a past that she wanted to put behind her. Florida was what she wanted, it was the place she saw herself building a new life, especially since most of the drama had been taken care of.

She wasn't sure what would happen if things didn't work out between her and Sage. She supposed one of them would have to move out eventually. She didn't like the thought, so she tried not to linger on it too much. She knew she would be fine if that did happen, but with how she felt about him, she hoped it wouldn't get to that. The thought of being without Sage had almost killed her once before, and she didn't need to let herself think of it when the likelihood of it happening was slim.

She had given up on a lot of things in her life when she had been growing up, always thinking of whether or not it was worth it at all. She had made so many mistakes and had taken so many wrong turns, she found it almost hard to believe that everything had led her to where she was. She never would've thought for one moment that even when her life had gone terribly wrong, she could manage to bring it back onto the right path.

She had had a few suicidal thoughts when she had been stuck in her late teens. She had considered ending it all because she had allowed herself to go so far from her dream. She knew back then that the possibility of reaching her dreams was so far out of reach, but she was glad she had survived through it all. It led her to something greater. She shivered at the thought of what she would've missed out on if she hadn't stuck through some of the hardest parts of her life. She wouldn't have Sage and that thought made her a bit sad.

Mia had made so many mistakes; she had, after all, almost killed herself unintentionally when she got involved with drugs. The more she thought about it, the more apparent things became about why she did what she did. She had gotten involved with drugs because it had dulled the feeling of failure that had lived inside her for so long. She had failed herself and her family when she had run away, and she knew she hadn't taken drugs just because she had an addictive personality but because she wanted to run away from herself altogether. Obviously, that didn't work; it almost killed her. And then she had gotten involved with the Omens, fully aware of what might happen to her if she failed them, but she was on a path of self-destruction at that stage. Even though a part of her wanted a better life, she still knew getting involved with the Omens was not the right choice for that. After all, she had almost gotten killed then too.

She believed she could almost have it all now as things were looking up for her. She could have Sage, who was slowly warming up to her and showing her in his own way that he wanted her too. He wouldn't say the words outright, but Mia knew that everything he had said and done to keep her away meant almost nothing. It still hurt her when she thought about how he had treated her not so long ago, but after everything they had been through together, she could see he was starting to change toward her.

When she had almost lost him, she decided to let go of all the things he had done. She couldn't hold it against him because she knew that it wouldn't be fair. Although he hadn't said sorry for it, his actions spoke louder. He had been the one who had done what he could to get them back to Florida, and she was grateful for that.

She knew Sage was impacting her life, and he had started to make her life seem brighter than it had for a long time. Just being around him made her want to melt, but it was more than just physical, she just wanted him as a whole. She wanted to give herself to him in a way she had never given herself before. Something that was new and scary for her to think about. She wasn't sure just how involved in her life Sage would get nor did she know if he would ever truly open up to her but regardless of that she wanted to make sure that he knew he could always rely on her. Being there for others had always been something Mia tried to do. She tried to give her best and always wanted to be someone people could go to when they needed a friend and in the end if all things failed she would still try to be a friend to Sage.

Mia made her way to her painting room. She had been looking forward to picking up her brushes the most. She had an overload of emotions that she wanted to release. She wanted to paint the excitement she felt that now filled her life again. She knew her life was changing, changing so that she felt as if light and happiness would ooze out of her pores so everyone could see. She felt more like herself now that she had somewhere to call her own. It had been something she had wished for for a long time.

The demons from her past had always seemed to follow her, casting a shadow over almost everything she did. She constantly tried to better her life, making things right with the universe, so to speak. She knew she had fucked up a lot of things, and a part of her regretted the fact that she had let her family go. They were all she had for sixteen years of her life, and she knew that although they hadn't gotten on that well, there was so much of her current life that she wished she could share with them. Whenever she would get married, she would have no one to walk her down the aisle, and she knew that it was her fault. She was always hard on herself, never wanting anyone to really see how much she had hurt the life she could've had, but now with everything getting better by the day, Mia had to realize that everything had worked out perfectly in the long run. Of course, she knew it wouldn't be easy but she would do whatever it took to make sure her life continued on the right path.

She had run away from most things in her life, fearing her destiny and never fully being able to commit to achieving the goals she had set out for herself but with the Hell Kats and the Screaming Demons in her life, she felt like she could do anything and for the most part, she would also do anything for those she cared about most. Fiona seemed to trust her again, making her feel like she was part of the Screaming Demons. Mia believed she had proved herself a few times, pushing herself to do things she had never done before, but she knew she would do it over again in a heartbeat, especially if it meant having Sage at her side.

With Fiona back on her side, she knew she was almost unstoppable. She could also see that Fiona trusted her with more, and she would prove herself worthy every day if she had to.

She picked up a blank canvas and began to paint. In her mind, all she could see was Sage, and so she decided she would paint him in all his glory. The love she had for him continued to grow in her chest the more she thought of him, and the more he spent time with her, she was dying to say those three words to him, but she held it back knowing that only when the time was right, she would tell him.

She started with a dark setting, black clouds looming over the city. In her mind's eye, she could see the view of the city from where Sage had taken her after she had confessed to working with the Omens. She knew that it was then that her life had started to turn around, and with the involvement of Sage, it had made things better for her. With Sage by her side, she knew she could do just about anything. He had only been in her life for a few days when she felt like she could trust him with her life. It was a huge thing letting someone in, especially for Mia because she had been so dependent on herself for so long.

She painted the skyscrapers covered in a dark cloud with the warnings of a thunderstorm, slightly blurring the edges with yellow to indicate the storm was coming. Mia let herself go as she painted. It shocked her when she stepped back and took a closer look at the painting. She had been so close to losing it altogether when she looked at how dark she had made the painting.

Mia knew she was drawing her life and how it had always seemed to be covered in darkness, threatening to crumble around her at any moment, but she placed Sage right at the corner of the painting. Although he was not the main focus of the picture, she covered him with light representing the light he had brought into her life. She didn't want to admit that it was all thanks to Sage that her life had finally turned around, but she knew deep down that if he hadn't made her come clean, she wouldn't have become a proper part of the Screaming Demons. She could've been dead if it wasn't for him, which is why she would constantly make sure he was safe too. She owed him her life.

She smiled to herself as she painted him to life. His broad shoulders and messy hair, she thought about how much he could carry on them and how much he already had. She wished she could help him lessen the load he carried with him from his past but knew that unless he was willing to let her in completely, that would never happen. She could almost see the weight he carried on his shoulders every time he moved. He walked tall and proud, but she could always see a slight slumped-ness to his shoulders, and she longed to change that. Mia knew that whatever he had gone through while in the army couldn't have been easy. It wouldn't be easy for anyone and although Sage was strong she felt that he would probably feel a lot better if he opened up more about his experiences.

She knew a lot of what had happened to him was the reason behind why he acted the way he did, why he seemed to shut her out sometimes. It wasn't because he didn't care about her and she knew that it was more because he had kept everything in for so long he didn't want to let anyone else in, but she noticed that he had started to change toward her.

It gave her hope for the future, of her future and most importantly, their future. She wasn't sure if anything would happen between them, but the possibility seemed promising.

She wanted him to know that she would be by his side no matter what happened and that she was someone he could rely on.

Mia stepped back to look at her painting, admiring her work and admiring Sage at the same time. She didn't want to paint him anymore, she wanted to be with him. She placed her brushes back in the jar she had set aside for them and headed to her shower. As usual, she had gotten paint all over herself in the process; she never had been a clean painter.

She walked to her room and headed for her shower, grabbing a towel on the way. She switched the water on and quickly cleaned herself up, wanting to be with Sage as soon as she possibly could. Her mind drifted to Sage while she was in the shower. Her mind seemed to drift to him almost every time she didn't concentrate on something else. He was back with her, in her arms and occasionally in her bed too. It was more than she had longed for and she was extremely happy about it. She felt a sense of happiness and belonging she hadn't felt before.

She finished in the shower so she could be with Sage. Thinking about him had made the need for him that much stronger. She wanted to be with him as quickly as possible. Once out of the shower and dressed in clean pajamas, Mia made her way to Sage. The lights in the house were off, so she assumed he was already in bed. She entered his room and saw him asleep, cuddled up under his blankets like a child. He seemed so different when he slept, so vulnerable, so childlike, it made her heart melt a little more. Getting into his bed, Mia shifted his arms and wrapped them around her.

"Are you joining me tonight?" Sage asked in a sleepy voice, obviously waking up from her moving him.

"Shh, go back to sleep," she replied in a hushed voice. She hadn't meant to wake him up.

"Sweet dreams," he said softly before drifting back to sleep. He pulled her closer to him, and within no time they were both fast asleep in each other's arms.

14

Once Sage and Mia had arrived back in Florida, Sage had to get straight back into work. He had to make sure that everything had gone alright while he had been away and he also had to make sure that they had their steps covered. He couldn't risk anything else going bad, and because of the mess the Omens had made, he knew he had to be fully aware of things.

Although he had known long before what the Omens did, he knew that it would've looked sketchy from the outside when the Omens stopped being so well known around the area. He just wished it hadn't gotten as far as it had. He wished he could change how things had played out; he would have tried to make the transition less noticeable. The Omens were huge in Florida, which was one of the reasons he was sent there. He had to take care of them, but he had to do it in a less obvious way.

He had slipped with a few things, but he couldn't allow that to happen again.

It had been hard on him when he thought about the mess he had made. He felt guilty and ashamed of himself when he remembered that he had caused everyone to get distracted by him being missing. If he hadn't let himself slip up, he wouldn't have been in that well in the first place, and someone would've seen the law enforcement officers sooner. He tried not to linger on the past. There wasn't much anyone could do about it. He just had to try to do better next time which was why he had to make sure he didn't make any more mistakes.

He had been so distracted after he was rescued, he didn't notice the law enforcement officers until it was too late and he couldn't risk that happening again. The fact that they had gone unnoticed in the first place sent off warning signs in Sage's mind. He had no idea how long they had been watching them before he had noticed them.

It was lucky that Sage and Mia didn't do much at the house besides leading a normal life. If he had been doing business at the house, things could've been a lot worse than they were. He wondered if they had been sitting outside the house watching Mia when he hadn't been around. He tried his hardest not to picture them possibly harming her when she had been all alone. He wouldn't have been able to live with himself if they had tried to do anything to her, like arrest her forcefully.

He decided to place a few secret cameras around the house. He wished he had done it sooner so he could've watched back the footage, but now would still work for future reference. He made sure they were not visible to anyone on the outside, but it gave him a sense of reassurance as he made sure his house was protected. Mia didn't ask him what he was doing when she saw him fiddling around the house. She left him to do what he needed to do, and he was thankful for that as he didn't want to alarm her. He placed a monitor in his office so he could keep a close eye on whatever happened outside. It would help him sleep at night. He also wanted to make sure Mia was protected. She had almost killed a few people trying to get him back, and she had witnessed way too much even before that. Sage didn't want her to go through anything else that could cause her harm.

He knew Mia was curious about what he did late at night when he didn't leave his office to join her for dinner, but she didn't ask him about that. Instead, she just made sure he had food ready and waiting. She was extremely thoughtful, letting him go about his business without bugging him was something he liked about her.

A few days after they got back to Florida, Sage knew he needed to spend some alone time with Mia. He had been extremely busy with work and he had hardly spent any time with her, and he felt terrible about it. She had been trying so hard to make things easy for him, making sure the house was clean and that he was always fed when he didn't have enough time to cook, which he never did, even to begin with. He remembered a place Adam had told him about once when they had been out on a job. It was a beach just a little bit out of the city. Apparently, it was never really busy, and it had a great view of the sunset. Sage thought it would be the perfect place to go with Mia. He was sure she would appreciate a beautiful sunset. Maybe one day she could paint a picture for him to see.

He really wanted to get to know Mia more. He had learned a lot about her by just being around her, but he wanted the chance to talk to her so they could bond more on a deeper level. She wasn't a hard person to crack as she wore her heart on her sleeve, but she held a certain amount of mystery that he found alluring. He knew he had fought his feelings for her for so long and although there were things about her he had picked up along the way, he wanted to also let her know that he was more open to the idea of them being together. He wasn't sure what he was ready for, but he was willing to give it a shot.

It was early in the morning when he went to find her in her room. She hadn't slept with him the night before because he had been up late in his office doing work. He had noticed that she had sometimes started to sneak into his room at night to sleep with him. He could half picture her doing it although sometimes he had thought he was dreaming until he would wake up with her there. He honestly loved waking up next to her, her arms wrapped around him while she would press her body as tightly against his as possible. She was definitely a safe haven for him.

He had gotten used to how her skin felt and how her hair smelled, it was almost one of those smells that bring you instant happiness like when you remember what your favorite sweet smelt like growing up. She felt like comfort to him, and he had longed for something like that for a long time.

She looked so peaceful as she was still sleeping, tucked away in her bed with her blanket wrapped around her tightly, clearly missing Sage next to her. He just watched her for a while, taking her in. He wanted to climb into her bed with her and hold her for a while but decided not to. He wanted to spend the day with her awake so he could get to know her better and so their bond could grow.

He walked over to her and gently shook her to wake her up. It wasn't too early so he didn't think it would be a problem, although he did notice she liked to sleep in if they didn't have to do anything in the morning.

"Mia, have a shower and get dressed. We're going out," he said. She groaned in her sleep as she started to come to. Sage noted that she may not be a morning person at all.

Mia rubbed at her eyes, forcing herself to open them before she was ready to wake up on her own. She didn't seem to be angry or upset at the sudden wake-up call, so he was in the clear of any angry words being thrown around.

"Huh? What time is it?" she asked in a sleepy voice. Sage couldn't help but think that she could be the cutest person he had ever seen wake up.

He had had his fair share of women before. He wouldn't call himself a man whore, but he had been sexual with a few women in his life. He wasn't exactly young anymore though, and as he looked at Mia, he found himself picturing them waking up together for a long time going forward. It was a picture he rather liked.

He could picture them waking up together for the rest of his life, and although the thought was scary, he couldn't fight it. His feelings for her had grown just by being around her, and because he had stopped trying to push her away, he could see all the great qualities she had.

"It's 8 am, and it's time for us to take on the day," he replied. He was eager to get out of the house as soon as he could. He'd been going a bit stir crazy as the days had passed with all the work he had been doing.

"Hmm, coffee. First coffee," she said as she sat up and started to stretch. Sage watched as she brought her arms over her head at stretched them upward as if she were trying to touch the ceiling, her eyes still closed.

"Okay, okay. I'll go do that, and you wake up," he said as he got up and left the room to make her coffee. He went to the kitchen, and while he made her a cup of coffee, he thought about where he would take her first. He knew a coffee wouldn't do, and he wasn't sure if there would be any places near the beach where they could have breakfast. He knew Mia loved having breakfast, and she would often make him eat with her if he was still around while she would be cooking. He quickly looked up a few cafes that were in the area and decided they would go out for breakfast first before they headed to the beach. He wanted to spend as much time as possible with Mia without there being any distractions.

He took Mia her coffee and told her about the day he had planned. She sat quietly in bed and listened while he spoke, her face completely passive.

"I think it would be good for us to have a bit of downtime together. I've been so busy since we've been back," he said.

Mia finally smiled.

"It would be lovely to spend some time with you. Let me have a shower, and then we can go," she replied.

Sage knew she was likely to agree to the idea, but he had been nervous to ask her, thinking that maybe their time apart had made her feel differently toward him. He was glad to know that he was just overthinking it. He left her room to allow her to get ready while he waited patiently in the lounge.

About 30 minutes later, Mia emerged dressed in a light blue blouse and a pair of jeans that hugged her curves in all the right ways paired with a black pair of boots.

"You look beautiful," Sage said as he looked at her for a while. A slight blush covered Mia's cheeks, and she slightly giggled. The one thing he loved about her was the fact that she hardly wore any makeup. She seemed to embrace her natural beauty all the time, and she definitely was amazingly beautiful.

"Thank you, you look rather handsome yourself," she replied. Sage was dressed in a pair of black jeans and a navy blue shirt. He had tried to make an effort.

"Thank you. Now let's get out of here," he said as he took her hand and led her out of the house. He led her to his bike where he handed over a helmet. He remembered that she hadn't been on his bike since the drive down to Florida and he smiled to himself at the memory.

"What are you smiling at?" Mia asked as she noticed the smile on his face.

"I'm just remembering the last time you were on my bike. That trip was torture with you constantly trying to tease me," he said as he mimicked her stretching.

"You knew the whole time?" she asked, shocked. Sage could tell she thought he didn't know what she was doing back then.

"Of course, I knew," he said.

"I thought I was being so clever," she said with a small laugh.

"You were being clever and extremely cheeky," he replied with a chuckle. "You're a very distracting woman even when you're not trying."

Mia blushed and quickly placed her helmet on to hide it, but Sage already saw and smiled to himself.

They climbed onto the bike and left the house. As Sage took off, he took a quick scan of outside the house and was happy to see no law enforcement vehicle parked outside. He was pleased that the work he had done had helped in the long run. He knew he could enjoy his day with Mia without any worries.

Sage hadn't spent any one-on-one time with anyone for such a long time. He had tried to separate himself from those around him ever since the military because he didn't want to have to go through losing anyone again. When he thought back to that time it wasn't just that he had lost Laura, but he had lost a group of friends too. They were more than friends, they had been his family too. They had shared so much together, and their bonds had grown when they fought alongside each other. It wasn't just that he hadn't pictured himself with another woman, but he had spent years making sure he never got too close to anyone.

That had all changed though when Mia was constantly by his side. He found it easier to let himself go around her. He felt like he could be more himself than he had been in a long time. He wasn't healed from his past and of course, the likelihood of him ever being completely healed was too far fetched, but he felt something for Mia that made him smile and feel more at peace around her.

It didn't take Sage too long to find the cafe he had found in his search. He was happy with his choice because the cafe was cute and arty with cakes and pastries of all kinds to choose from.

He stopped the bike and hopped off, stretching his arm out so Mia could take his hand as she got off the bike behind him.

"This is so cute!" Mia exclaimed as she looked at the cafe. Sage was pleased with himself. He was glad he had known something about Mia's taste.

"I'm glad I chose correctly; I thought you'd like it," he replied.

They headed into the cafe. Both were greeted by a small chubby woman with bright red hair who directed them to a table and took their orders. They had a bit of small talk as they waited for their food, but the place was still quiet enough for the time of the day, so it didn't take long for their food to arrive. Within an hour, they were back on the bike and on their way for the next activity of the day.

It didn't take them long to arrive at the beach, and Sage knew instantly that it had been a perfect choice. They walked along the beach for a while with their shoes in their hands so their toes could sink into the sand beneath them. It was relaxing and peaceful as the beach was empty while they walked. Sage was grateful for the moment. He was grateful that Mia was by his side to share it with him. He had given her so many chances to walk away from him when he had tried to push her away, but she was a force of nature and would not settle for anything less than what she wanted. He was glad he was something she saw an interest in. He couldn't imagine what his life would be like without her.

They sat down after a while, and because there was a slight breeze in the air, they sat close together, feeling the warmth of each other's body heat. It felt good for both of them; it felt right.

Sage didn't think about much while they sat there, enjoying the view that was before them. His mind didn't wander back to his past, nor did he find himself trying to pull away. However, he felt at peace for the first time in a long time. He looked at Mia while she had her eyes closed, her face tilted toward the sun, and she looked breathtaking. She was so beautiful that Sage almost reached over so he could gently kiss her, but instead he just watched her. She seemed to smile softly as the breeze tickled her face. It had been a long time for both of them since they had been out of the house and still in each other's company. He could picture them going to the beach more often to get a break from work. It could be a new tradition they created for themselves as a couple. Sage smiled at the thought.

"It's so beautiful," Mia said as she opened her eyes and looked across the ocean. She watched the waves gently crash into each other. The smell of the ocean filled their noses, salty and fishy but still refreshing. They had been in the city for so long that a change in scenery was what they needed to get their minds off of the problems that had happened recently, even if it was just for the moment. The amount of drama that had happened recently had started to take a toll on both of them.

"It's hard to concentrate on the beauty of the sea when I'm sitting here next to you," Sage replied. He had continued to watch her out of the corner of his eye since they had sat down. Her hair gently floated around her face, shifting with the breeze that pricked at their faces.

"When did you become so soppy?" she asked teasingly as she gently nudged him with her elbow. It was a question Sage couldn't answer because he knew that deep down it had been since he had met her.

For him, there had been no other explanation for how he had started to act when she entered his life. He had never tried to force someone out of his life the way he had tried with her, but even when he had thought it was the right thing to do, there had been a part of him that still wanted her near.

"You've made it extremely hard to ignore you, you know," he replied. He didn't want to hold anything back from her. He knew he wouldn't go into his past, but he could still talk about how she made him feel in his life right now.

"I told you I always work hard for what I want, Sage," she said. He believed her, she had managed to grab his attention from the beginning, and he wanted to know everything there was to know about her. He hadn't allowed himself to feel anything for anyone in a long time so it was almost overwhelming to him that since Mia had appeared in his life, he really couldn't stop thinking about her.

"What are some things you want?" he asked.

"Well, I guess I've always wanted to be an artist

which you already know, but I'd really like that to be a reality and not just a dream."

"Why don't you showcase some of your work?" he replied. He hadn't managed to see any of her work yet, but with how long she had started to spend painting in the office, he could only imagine how good she was.

"I'm terrified of people judging it and telling me that I'm not good enough. I'm so passionate about painting that I'm worried that with the wrong criticism I could stop altogether and I really don't want that to happen," she said.

He could tell she was serious, the look on her face showed just how scared she was.

"Can you show me your work some time?" he asked.

Mia thought about it for a while, wriggling her nose as she thought.

"Maybe one day. And what about you, what do you want?" she asked.

"I think I wouldn't mind a clean slate in some areas of my life. There are so many things I wish I could forget but never will," he replied as he thought back to his experience in Afghanistan. He wished he could forget it all.

"You mean from the army?" Mia asked. He knew she would pick up on the hint, she was a smart woman.

"Yeah, I mean it was an experience that I'm half grateful for, but it's been tough since then," he replied.

He knew he wouldn't go into too much detail, but he was finding it easy to talk to her about it. They were bonding over life, and it was making them that much closer.

"I'm sure that kind of thing wouldn't be easy for anyone, but you know sometimes it's good to talk about it, and if you wanted to I could listen," she replied. Sage appreciated her offer, but he knew it would be a while before he opened up completely about what had happened while in the army.

"Thank you, Mia. It means a lot to me," he said.

They sat in silence for a while.

"What do you paint?" he asked. He wouldn't push her to show him her work if she wasn't ready to share it, but he was still interested to know what she spent so much time on.

"It's mostly in the moment, it's usually how I'm feeling and what I'm thinking at that time so it could be anything. Sometimes it's nothing at all but just a lot of different colors meshed together," she replied. Sage watched her as she spoke, her hands lifted from the sides of her body as she used them to stroke the sky, making out the motions she used when she painted. He watched and pictured a paintbrush in her hands. She seemed so gentle but sure of her movements as her hands moved. It was captivating.

Sage took Mia's hand in his as it started to get colder.

Her hand was soft and cold against his. They made no effort to leave the beach.

"You know, I've never held a guy's hand before," Mia said as she looked down at their hands intertwined. It wasn't that surprising to Sage as he had already learned about her dating history. He found it sad that no one had truly loved her before. It was almost impossible for him not to love her, so how could anyone else ignore the amazing person she was.

He wondered what she thought about herself if she didn't value herself that much. Sometimes when Sage would watch her, he could tell she was unsure about herself and he wanted her to see how amazing she truly was. His past had changed the way he saw people around him, but her past had changed the way she saw herself, and he really wanted her to know that she was a lot more than what she viewed herself to be.

She had shown him countless times just how strong she was, and the way she presented herself was always in a respectful manner, but when she walked into a room, everyone would stop and watch her. She demanded attention without even knowing it. It was just because of the way she was. She never asked for anyone to look at her, nor did she try too hard, but she had a way about her that people just couldn't ignore. The Screaming Demons respected her which was why she had been made one and all the girls in the Hell Kats looked up to her. She was powerful and for some reason, Sage knew she didn't actually know that.

She deserved so much more than what she had gotten most of her life, from the men she had allowed in, and if anything, Sage wanted to show her what she could have and so much more.

## 15

Mia had enjoyed spending time with Sage. Not only was the beach the perfect place to spend some time alone together but it was so beautiful too. She wished she had had a canvas with her so she could have captured the moment when the sun set and the colors in the sky changed. It was breathtaking, and as an artist, it was something she could never forget.

She knew that when she had the chance she would paint it. It wasn't just because it was beautiful but because she had been able to share a wonderful moment with Sage after they had been missing each other. Even with living together, sometimes they wouldn't spend time together. Mia hadn't realized how much she had missed being with Sage. She had worried that maybe he had started to pull away from her for a reason, but she had also been sneaking into his room at night which he hadn't complained about, so she knew she had been overthinking it in the end.

Being with him had reassured her of the feelings she had for him. He opened up a little to her, and she was grateful for just that little bit of trust he showed to her. They hadn't really spoken about their lives besides the night they went out of the city back in Pine Hill, so it was good to have the chance to talk openly again.

The time they had spent together was also almost magical. It felt as if they were in their own world as they sat on the beach and talked. They opened up to each other about a few things, and Mia wanted to tell Sage how she felt. The words had almost slipped out of her mouth at one point, but she knew better than to say them then. She knew Sage wasn't ready for that yet, but she was happy he had made an effort with her. She also knew that because she hadn't loved a man before, it was a huge step for her too. She wanted to be extra careful that he showed that he could feel the same before she said the words she had been dying to say. They had been so separated lately that she had hardly seen him awake most days since they had gotten back from Pine Hill so she hoped they could spend more time together so she could truly see how he felt about her.

There hadn't been much for her to do though, so she had spent a lot of her time painting and watching TV which she didn't mind so much. It gave her the chance to unwind after everything that had happened recently. She also started shopping online for groceries and for paintings and things she could place around the house. Sage had taken it upon himself to do a lot of work. It was clear he was trying to make up for the two days he had been out of action although no one held it against him at all. They had told him to slow down a few times because he had been pushing himself, but he refused to listen. Mia didn't bother trying to tell him what to do.

The day at the beach wasn't just perfect because of all of that but also because they went to bed together, both awake and aware of the time they got to be together. It had been more intimate than sex. He held her as they slept, their bodies intertwined as they dreamed. Her feelings for Sage were stronger than ever, and she believed Sage felt the same. They had slept together a few times, but mostly when one of them snuck in during the night while the other was sleeping. It seemed to be an unspoken rule that they would constantly just want to be with each other at night. They had talked a bit before they had fallen asleep, laughing and snuggling against each other as the day came to a close. Mia slept better when she was with Sage.

*"I'm so proud of you," a gentle voice said from behind Mia. She knew instantly that it belonged to her mother, and when she turned to face her, tears welled in her eyes. Her mother*

*looked older, fragile, but still as beautiful as she had when Mia had last seen her. She was a bit confused as to what her mother was saying, but as she took a look around her, she noticed some of her paintings on the walls.*

*She was in an art gallery, and she was exhibiting her work. Mia was shocked because even with her passion for painting and art, she never pictured herself being part of an exhibition.*

*Her paintings looked different compared to how she had been painting. They were more detailed, and all of them were of Sage. Some were just his eyes, and others were just different areas of his body, one of his arms, his shoulders, his jawline. As she turned around the room and took in all of her work, she spotted Sage in the far corner of the room. Nervously she walked toward him. Her cheeks went red as he looked at her and smiled. She felt exposed and slightly embarrassed by her work.*

*"This is amazing," he said as she stood next to him. He took her hand and laid a kiss on her palm.*

*"You don't think it's too much?" she asked as she saw Sage in all angles around them.*

*"It's not about what you capture, it's about how you capture it, and I must say you captured me extremely well," he replied with a small squeeze of her hand. Mia smiled as she was relieved he didn't find it overwhelming.*

*"Well, you've captured my heart," she said as she looked into his eyes. Leaning forward, he gently kissed her cheek.*

*"You've captured mine, it's all yours," he replied. She could tell he was telling the truth, she could almost see through his skin and saw how his heart beat for her.*

Mia smiled in her sleep. The day at the beach had made her feel connected to Sage more than ever. They had talked openly about things, and she didn't feel like he would judge her for what she said. Her dreams revolved around Sage that night, playing out different situations in her head that always had him confessing his feelings toward her.

She woke up feeling refreshed and more alive than she had for a long time. She felt as if anything was possible. She was in a daze most of the day as she attended to the house and found herself painting more of Sage. She didn't paint him as she had in her dream, but she decided to paint his face. It was after all her favorite thing about him.

It didn't take long for that to come to a halt when she received a call from the Hell Kats in the late afternoon.

Lorraine was back at the club, drunk and shouting things at people. Mia knew she would have to go down there herself and sort it out. She couldn't believe Lorraine was back after they had told her to leave. She was clearly asking for trouble, practically begging for it. Mia couldn't understand why she would act like that. No one in their right mind would want people to see them in that way. She was making a fool of herself, and her behavior was not only unwanted but unnecessary. The Screaming Demons club wasn't for people who just wanted to get drunk, it was a community place where friends who were family would get together. Lorraine was unwelcome if she wasn't going to act like a normal person.

"I have to go to the club and sort something out," she told Sage as she was heading for the door. "I shouldn't be too long." She was frustrated and irritated that her peaceful day had been ruined. It was clear that Lorraine was a bigger problem than she had thought.

"What's going on?" Sage asked. She didn't want him to worry, but she couldn't lie to him either.

"Lorraine is back, drunk and causing a scene at the bar," she replied.

"Do you need me to come with you?" he asked. She liked that he worried about her, but she could handle it without having him getting involved. After all, she had been the one that had been called, which made it her responsibility.

She couldn't believe that taking care of a drunk person had become her duty, but she knew that because she was a woman, it would be easier for her to solve the problem.

"I've got this covered. If I need you, I'll give you a call," she replied. She knew she wouldn't call him, though, she could handle it on her own.

"Okay, be safe," he called as she headed to the door.

"I will," she called back. She knew that the only person who should be safe was Lorraine. Mia could look after herself. She was strong enough to handle whatever was placed in front of her.

She called a cab and made her way to the club. She really didn't want to have to deal with Lorraine again. The task had been so taxing the first time she had tried to talk to her. She had had a feeling when she first met her that she would be a problem, but she really didn't want to have to go back and forth from her house and the club to deal with her.

We really need to get a car, she thought to herself. As much as she loved riding the bike and she liked that Sage had given her permission to use his, she didn't want to ride it all the time, but neither of them had gotten around to getting a car. She would have to do that as soon as possible if problems with Lorraine kept happening. She really hoped this would be the last time she would have to deal with her though.

Mia couldn't understand why Lorraine had come back. Everyone knew that the Hell Kats meant business and because Mia was also a Screaming Demon that should also mean something. No one should think they can just come into the club and cause problems. It had to be stopped and the fact that she had already been told the first time just made the situation worse. She was not doing what she was told, and she underestimated Mia. Mia would eventually have to show her that she wouldn't stand by and just let her do as she pleased.

She arrived at the bar and entered through the doors. She noticed all the Hell Kats were standing around the bar, crowding around someone. As she got closer, she could see that they were all standing around Lorraine who was slurring and yelling at anyone who paid her any attention. She didn't have any real sense of herself as she swayed on the barstool, hardly managing to stay seated as she turned this way and that way while she yelled at people near her. She was looking for attention, which she clearly wasn't getting as her voice rose higher.

Mia walked up to her and sat down next to her. She noticed a few shot glasses were lined up in front of her. Picking one up, Mia could smell the tequila. It was clear she had at least six tequila. It could've been more, of course.

"Hello, Lorraine. I thought I told you to leave and not come back," she said. It took a while for Lorraine to focus on her. She was completely drunk, and it wasn't even dark yet. It was pathetic.

"Oh, it's *you*," she said, "little miss perfect. Well, you know what he'll come back to me when he's bored of you which will happen soon enough. Just look at you, you're nothing special," she slurred as she pointed at Mia who had no idea what she was talking about. It didn't make sense to her at all.

"I'm not surprised that you've been left by a man considering you're already drunk at this time," Mia replied. It was possible that in her drunken state Lorraine thought she was someone else, someone who had taken her man. She pitied the woman, but it wasn't enough to justify her actions.

"He's mine, he'll always be mine," she continued as if Mia hadn't spoken at all. It was possible that she could be a raging alcoholic, no one who was happy with life would be drunk before 6 pm.

"Come on, let's get you home. Where do you live?" Mia asked. She wrapped one arm under Lorraine and guided her out of the bar. Reluctantly she gave Mia her address. It wasn't her responsibility to take her home, and she could've asked some of the Hell Kats to do it, but a part of her wanted to make sure that she got home safely without having to rely on someone else doing the job.

Mia put her in a cab and climbed into the front seat, giving the driver the address. She would make sure she got home safely, even if that meant putting her to bed herself. Lorraine sat in the back of the cab and continued to talk. Most of her words came out slurred, and Mia struggled to understand her, but she kept repeating, 'he's mine, he's mine,' as they got closer to her house.

"Who are you talking about?" Mia asked, frustrated with the woman when she refused to shut up.

"You know, you know," Lorraine replied.

"You definitely need to sleep this off," Mia said as she got Lorraine out of the back seat of the cab once they had arrived outside her house. "Where are your house keys?"

"Pocket," was all Lorraine replied as she started to hiccup.

Mia searched her pockets for her keys and unlocked the front door once she found them. She carried Lorraine inside and placed her on the couch she saw in the lounge. She didn't have the strength or energy to take her to her room. She covered her with a blanket and decided that she would have a real chat with her the next day. She would have to tell her again that she needed to move on and stop showing up at the club like she had been told. It wasn't just because she was drunk but because of everything else she had done already. She had seemed like trouble from the get-go and Mia had to protect the club.

Once she had Lorraine settled, she headed home. She wanted to be with Sage. When she arrived home, she found Sage in his study working.

"Isn't it a bit late to be working still?" she asked.

"Work never stops, but I was just about to take it easy for the rest of the night. Shall we go watch some TV?" he replied.

"Why, I like the way you think," she said.

They made their way to the lounge and curled up on the couch together.

"Have you eaten anything for dinner?" she asked as she took notice of the time. It was still early, and Mia had begun to feel a bit hungry.

"I haven't now that you mention it. Shall we cook up something quickly and then continue watching the movie?" he asked.

"That sounds like a plan," she replied. They got up and headed to the kitchen.

Together they made dinner, laughing and messing around while they did. They seemed to be getting to a good point in their relationship, a place Mia had never been before with anyone in her past.

Mia had always wanted someone to love her for who she was, and she longed for someone to give her the chance for her to love them back. She had a big heart that had been through so much, and she knew she had a lot of love to give, and the more time she spent with Sage her hopes of them having some sort of future grew.

## 16

Spending more time with Mia started to change the way Sage saw things. Their relationship hadn't been easy, but they were on a path that he hadn't been down for a long time, and even though it was scary for him, he wouldn't want it any other way. There was so much he wanted to learn about Mia, but already he knew he couldn't be without her going forward. He had tried his hardest to keep them separated, not wanting to get too close to her because his biggest fear was losing people. That was starting to change for him. She had been fighting for him and alongside him for a while and to him, it just proved how sure she was of him. It made it easier for him to slowly let her in.

He knew he had pushed a lot of people away during his life. He had probably hurt more people than he had intended to, but he had tried to look out for himself. He couldn't afford to lose anyone after what he had been through, so he decided to not let anyone close enough to him. He knew it wasn't really the best decision to make or the best life to have, but it had served him well so far. Not many people knew it because of the way he presented himself, but Sage was a very emotional person, he always had been, but he had blocked his emotions off when he came back from the army. He should've seen someone about the trauma he had gone through. He wasn't stupid enough to believe ignoring it would make it go away, but he did what he could without seeking assistance.

He thought it would appear that he was weak if he asked for help. He was a military man, and he was strong enough on his own. Well, that's what he believed before Mia showed up. She showed that she would support him no matter what he went through, even if that meant he pushed her away in the process. He believed she had learned that he would always go back to her which surprisingly for him was true. He had never wanted to rely on anyone, and when he had been with Laura he had also tried to keep things away from her. Most of the time she hadn't tried too hard to get anything out of him. He wondered if it was because she didn't care or if she just wasn't interested in him the way he had thought she was.

They had been on a path to a future together, but maybe it had meant more to him than it had to her. He would never find that out, of course, but nevertheless, he believed she had loved him and a part of him had been looking for a partnership when he had met her, but it was different with Mia. He wanted so much more with her than he had ever expected. He would never have thought that a small person like her would have impacted his life this much in such a short period of time.

While they slept, Sage curled himself around Mia, cradling her body against his while he had a dreamless sleep. The dreams of Laura had started to slowly stop as his heart became more focused on Mia. It was a big thing for him. Although he hadn't told anyone about his dreams he knew that as long as he was letting Laura go, the dreams would stop eventually and while he continued to let Mia in, he became sure that he had made the right choice. He had to remind himself that Mia was what he had and Laura was in the past. He had to let her go so he could have a future. Whether it would be with Mia or not, he knew he deserved it.

He had had a lot of dark thoughts when he was in the well, but since then he had realized that he could have a better life and he had to live like that regardless. He didn't just owe it to himself, but he also owed it to his team. He had to give them something to be proud of, and he had to be proud of himself too. He knew he had made a lot of different decisions that had led him down a path they probably thought he wouldn't have gone, but he had worked hard to get to where he was and he was happy with the choice he had made.

He knew the only person he needed approval from was himself because he was the only one left, and the only person he answered to. It hadn't been easy when he had gone home. His mother had tried to look after him for months while his head healed, which had driven him crazy. When he finally had the chance to leave, he didn't turn back. It wasn't that he didn't appreciate all his mother had done for him, but he knew the longer he spent with her, the more he would have probably be driven to insanity. It sounded cruel, but she had babied him and had constantly made him feel as if he couldn't do anything with a head injury. She had stopped him from getting a few jobs, warning him that he wasn't ready. He had no choice but to leave it all behind when he found the job with Fiona. He knew his mother would never have been pleased with the choice and she wouldn't have accepted it.

Sage woke up with Mia in his arms. He held her there for a while, enjoying her body next to his. Although they hadn't had sex, Sage was enjoying his time with Mia, especially considering her presence helped him sleep better at night. It had been a long time since he had had any really bad dreams. His last bad dream had been just before his kidnapping. It was a relief to him as there were times when he had dreaded going to sleep because of those dreams. He didn't want to see anyone about them because he knew where that would lead him. He was glad they had started to go away on their own.

He wanted to stay there with her, but he knew he had to go to work. As much as his life had turned around, he couldn't stop doing what he needed to do. Grier relied on him, and he wanted to constantly show that he could do the jobs given to him. He had messed up so much recently so he felt he had something more to prove. He had to show that he was a part of the team more so than ever before.

He took a quick shower, slightly fantasizing about Mia but not allowing himself to think too much of it; she was just in the other room after all. He made himself a quick breakfast and had a cup of coffee before he left the house. He had to move some things from one shop to the other. Business never stopped, but he was happy he had spent some time with Mia. They had gotten to know each other just a little bit more, and he liked what he was learning. He stayed focused on work for the day, and as the day came to an end, he was happy to be heading home to Mia. The thought was definitely something that made him happy.

He knew his life had turned around with the help of Fiona and Grier. They had looked after him, they had looked after both him and Mia, and he could see the way it had changed Mia. Most importantly, they had given him a reason to live. He had been so busy being consumed by his past that he had almost given up on finding something that would turn him back onto the path he enjoyed. He knew not a lot of people would agree with what he did, especially because he was a military man, but he felt like his presence still protected people around him and to him that was all that mattered.

When he had come back to Pine Hill after the bombing in Afghanistan, he knew he would never go back to the army. It had damaged him far too much for him to think it could ever make his life better. He knew it shouldn't be about him but more about the fact that he was saving his country, but he had seen the inner workings of the military. The wars were too far gone for anything or anyone to be saved. It was too late for him to be completely saved too, but with Mia around, he felt like a part of him was slowly starting to heal, a part of him he had ignored for far too long.

Sage knew that although their lives had been placed together just out of coincidence, her being there for him was more than he could have ever asked for. Fiona had forced them to be together at the start, but he was grateful for it. Not only would he have probably died a few weeks ago if it wasn't for Mia, but her life had started to change because of him too. He would have to thank Fiona for her involvement one day. She would probably wink at him because he felt that she knew all along that they were bound to be together.

He laughed at the thought. If he had known that joining the Screaming Demons would have changed his life so drastically, he would've found them a long time ago. Maybe he wasn't ready back then, and it had all happened when it was supposed to happen. He liked to believe that everything happened for a reason. He knew he had met Mia so his life would find a new meaning even if he had thought he had lived his life as best as he could. She was something he hadn't seen coming, and when she was right there in front of him, he had still tried to deny it.

He knew she had been someone to watch out for. He had figured that out the moment he met her, but he wasn't sure if he could let her in. She had a personality that couldn't be ignored, and her laugh drove him crazy most of the time. Of course not being able to let her in wasn't personal and he wished he could explain that to her because he knew she wanted him to talk to her more, but he couldn't explain it without going into his history which he wasn't ready to do. He hated himself for the fact that he wasn't ready to talk about it. Most of the time it ate away at him on the inside because he could tell that she wanted to be there for him.

He didn't want to pass his bad life stories onto anyone else, especially considering nothing could change what had already happened and for the longest time that had been something he had to come to terms with. He could never go back and change what had happened in the past and in the end, it probably was the best thing for him. Even though his past was hard it had shaped him into the man he was. He had the future to look forward to, a future he had started feeling more positive about. He hadn't pictured much of a future for himself for a long time so it was rather refreshing to think about what could possibly happen in the future.

Sage spent some time trying to figure out what he could do that would show Mia just how much he cared about her. He definitely wasn't ready to talk about getting married nor was he ready to talk about having children. That would be a huge step that he wasn't one hundred percent ready for. The last time he had thought about something like that he had lost everything. He knew no one that surrounded him knew too much about his past. No one even knew that he had wanted to marry Laura. He had never discussed it with anyone back then, and he couldn't picture himself talking about it to anyone any time soon.

He also knew he wasn't ready to give them a title just

yet. That could be something they could talk about eventually, but for now, he wanted to show her that he valued her role in his life.

He felt like he belonged to her in some way, like they were tied together on some deeper level that he could never really explain to anyone, but he wanted everyone to know somehow. He had never had a bond with someone the way he had with her. Of course, he had gone through a lot of life and death situations with his team back when he was in the army, but it hadn't meant so much considering it was their job to expect it to happen. They were supposed to try to help save each other, but Mia didn't have to save him from the well. She could've just left him to rot once she had found out where he was. It still surprised him that she had even searched for him.

We could wear rings, he thought to himself, but that thought soon left his mind because that symbolized too much. He also didn't want to make a promise to her because he already knew he was committed to her. He wanted something that could last forever. He knew getting any sort of jewelry would be pointless because he hadn't seen Mia wear much since he'd met her.

A lot of thoughts crossed his mind, but none of them stuck until he thought of something so good not even he could deny the brilliance behind it. Some could say he was crazy but he knew that if anything it would be a true symbol of his feelings for Mia, it would be a way that he could express himself without having to do too much talking. He didn't care too much about what anyone else thought either. As long as Mia agreed he thought it was a perfect idea.

He had never gotten a tattoo before. He had never thought too much of it, but he felt it was an amazing way to bond with Mia, especially considering she was a creative person. He wasn't sure if she'd agree, but he hoped she would at least think about it. He wouldn't expect her to say yes right away and because it was such a huge step forward, he hoped she would see the true meaning behind it.

He made his way home to Mia with a huge smile on his face. He felt that his decision was the best idea he'd had yet. He knew some people were superstitious about tattoos, but he didn't believe in all of that nonsense. If it meant something to him and Mia, that was that mattered. He started to think about what he would get as he drove home, there were a few options, but he had to make sure that it symbolized Mia's character.

He arrived home and walked into the house, instantly smelling food being cooked. He had never met anyone who loved cooking as much as Mia did. He appreciated it a lot because he hardly thought of cooking himself food most days.

He had not exactly looked after himself well after the

army. He had his mother helping him for a while, but when he had been on his own he hardly cooked at all. He would mostly just order food, eat it straight out of the container it came in and then he'd throw it away. No mess, no fuss was what he used to say. It sounded sad when he thought about it, and from an outsider's perspective it probably was sad. At the time he was definitely sad, though he would never have admitted it to anyone.

When he had been on his own he had tried to stay clean. He kept his apartment clean and he made sure he had clean clothes, although he didn't exactly do the washing himself. He had a cleaner for that. He hated to admit it, but he had been dependent on anyone else who could take the burden of living off of him. He had tried to stay strong by going to the gym and working out so he could keep distracted from the mundane life he had led.

He walked into the kitchen and found Mia hunched over the kitchen counter. She was a sight for sore eyes, and it was so amazing to Sage that she cared so much for him to constantly make sure he had dinner even when he would be busy most of the day. He had never had someone who just wanted to look after him before, who just wanted to make sure he was fed. It pulled at his heartstrings when he realized that Mia truly cared for him and would take care of him. He hadn't been the most deserving person of that sort of treatment, and he knew it, so it meant the world to him. Seeing her there not only made him happy, but it reassured him that his idea was what he wanted to do. He was grateful he hadn't given up on life. Everything had led him to her. His eyes looked at her, memorizing her features as she moved around the kitchen completely unaware that he had come home.

"What's for dinner tonight?" he asked from behind her. He could bow down to her, he could lay his life on the line for her. She had honestly been the one thing that had saved him from himself. Even when he thought he had been surviving, he really hadn't now that he knew what his life could be like. He knew at that moment that he was allowing himself to really open himself up to her. One day he would tell her about his past.

"Beef and broccoli stir fry," she replied as she spun around to look at him. She smiled at him as she took him in. He too couldn't contain a smile as he looked at her. Mia looked gorgeous no matter what she was doing, and anyone would be blind not to see it. How she had gone through life without being snatched up already blew Sage's mind. Anyone would've been lucky to have a woman like her in their life. He could not let her go now.

"Yum, sounds delicious," he said.

"Well, even if it isn't I expect you to eat it all," she replied with a laugh. He had no doubt in his mind that it would taste amazing. One thing he had learned was that she was an amazing cook, no matter what she cooked. It could be as simple as cheese grilled sandwiches, and they would still taste amazing, gourmet even.

"Don't underestimate yourself, your food is always great," he said. He could picture them having a Sunday roast with a table filled with delicious food all cooked by Mia. He would, of course, offer to help but she would banish him from the kitchen. He knew she liked to cook alone.

"You're so kind. Can I pour you a drink while you wait?" she asked. He noticed that she was in hostess mode, aiming to please whoever was around her at all times.

"No, no. Let me pour you a drink. You'll maybe need it after what I have to say," he said.

"That sounds a bit scary," she replied.

"Not at all," he said as he poured her a small glass of wine. He knew in the back of his mind that if she agreed to go through with his idea, drinking too much wouldn't be a good idea.

"Okay, well, now that you've got me all nervous, tell me what's going on," she replied as she took the glass of wine into her hands.

"I thought about it a lot today or more so just a few

moments ago, but I thought that if you would be interested, maybe we could go get some tattoos tomorrow?" he asked. He could immediately see the shock on her face. He knew his idea seemed a bit crazy and out of nowhere, but it could be the perfect thing for them.

They weren't the materialistic type of people. They didn't need objects to make them happy, which was also one of the reasons why Sage thought tattoos would be the best option. Although Mia had made an effort around the house to make it look homier, he knew that if it came down to it, and as long as he had her by his side, he would be happy. There was no reason to hold on to material things considering when death came knocking, there would be nothing he could take with him.

Obviously, tattoos were pretty permanent, even getting a removal left a scar, but there was no part of him that could even think of getting a tattoo that meant something for Mia removed at a later stage. He was 100 percent sure he would be happy with it on him for the rest of his life, but if Mia didn't want to do it with him, he would still want to show her somehow just how much she meant to him and how serious he was about being with her. If she said no, he would think of something else he could do.

"Whoa, I don't know what to say to that," she replied.

"You don't have to give me an answer right away. You can think about it. I thought we could do something that symbolizes our bond," he said. He knew Mia was that type of person. She had to think everything through before she acted. He liked that about her. He could see the thoughts crossing her mind, he could see the calculating look in her eyes.

"Okay, okay. Um, alright. Sorry, I'm babbling, I just didn't expect that" she replied.

"Take your time to think about it. I'll give you all the time you need," he said.

"That would work, let me just think about it," she said with a smile. She turned back to the food and finished dinner. They sat in silence most of the dinner, which wasn't awkward as most people would think. They didn't seem to mind the silence while they were together. Sage watched Mia carefully for the rest of the night. She didn't give much away as the night went on. A bit of chit chat was exchanged, a general conversation about how their days had been. Once dinner was done they cleaned up and went to bed. Mia shared a bed with Sage more often, and so when they climbed into bed together, there wasn't any weirdness.

They laid in bed in silence for a while, both of them thinking of what the next day could hold. Tattoos, tattoos that would be with them for the rest of their lives. It was a scary thought, but Sage was extremely willing to do it, he knew in his heart it was right. Mia was right for him, they were right for each other.

## 17

Mia was completely shocked when Sage suggested that they get ink as a sign of their bond. She had wanted Sage, of course, but she had never thought about getting ink together. It seemed like a crazy idea. She had never thought that in her life she would get a tattoo with anyone, no matter who that person was but for some reason getting a tattoo with Sage seemed like something she wasn't against, and she knew it was because she loved him. She was still a bit hesitant about it though as not many people got tattoos for each other anymore because things are never guaranteed to last.

Even marriages didn't last forever. Mia knew that Sage was showing her in the only way he could think of that he wanted to be with her, that even though he couldn't yet talk about the future, he could still picture her there with him. It meant a lot to Mia the more she thought about it. It was a big gesture to make, even just having the courage to ask her must've taken a lot for him, and she was thrilled that the bond she had pictured forming between them wasn't just one-sided.

She went to bed with the idea of getting a tattoo on her mind. His idea ran through her mind over and over again. She kept thinking about what she would get if she did go through with it. She even thought about what he would get. She couldn't possibly think of an idea because he didn't give much away so it could literally be anything. Maybe he was thinking of getting her name she thought. She really hoped not though, that was just too much.

Mia knew that she wanted to be with Sage for the rest of her life. She had, of course, thought about it, but she never thought he'd want to get something so permanent.

She didn't want to give an answer straight away, so she decided to sleep on it. If he was willing to wait, he would have to give her enough time to really think about it. She was grateful he didn't push her into answering right away as getting a tattoo would be the biggest step they had taken together. She cuddled up next to Sage in her sleep, dreaming of getting his name branded on her. She shivered in her sleep at the thought. She knew without a doubt she would never get anyone's name tattooed on her, so she hoped that wasn't his idea.

*"How could you have made me get a tattoo of your name, and now you're leaving me?" she asked. Sage stood in front of her with his bags packed and waiting in the hallway of their house. She had known getting tattoos wouldn't make anything seem more real than it already was, getting tattoos with anyone didn't seal the deal.*

*"I'm sorry, Mia, I really am. You have to know that I didn't want this to happen. I thought we were doing something amazing," he replied. Mia looked at her tattoo. His name would be on her for the rest of her life, and he would just leave her life as if nothing mattered. Tears fell down her cheeks as she realized she hadn't been good enough to make him stay.*

*"Everyone always leaves," she said as she started to sob. Sage wrapped his arms around her and held her tight, but Mia couldn't take it and pushed him off of her.*

*"Just leave then. Just go and don't come back!" she yelled as frustration and anger filled her body. If he wanted to leave, he should. There was no reason why he should try to make it any better. He picked up his bags and walked out of the door. Not turning back to look at her, he just continued to walk forward and out of her life.*

Mia moaned in her sleep as the dream messed with her heart. It hurt to even think about Sage leaving her. She knew the idea of the tattoo had brought about the dream. It was a scary idea that she had never thought would come out of his mouth. She was terrified it could break their relationship in the long run. She knew a few people who had gotten tattoos with their partners and had broken up just a few months later. She didn't want that to happen to them.

"Good morning," Sage said from beside her as she woke up. He had a beautiful smile plastered on his face. Mia hoped she hadn't said anything embarrassing in her sleep, especially since there was a part of her that would've begged the Sage in her dreams to stay.

"Good morning to you too," she replied as she stretched. The best feeling in the world was waking up next to him, and it would never get old for her.

She was on her back and decided to turn so she could face him properly. There was no point in prolonging the question that hung in the air.

"So you're serious about getting a tattoo?" she asked. She wanted to make sure that he hadn't changed his mind overnight.

"Yes, I'm sure about getting a tattoo," he replied as he gently stroked her arm under the blanket.

"Isn't getting a tattoo together bad luck?" she asked him. She was concerned that it could break them before anything truly happened, thinking back to the dream she had just had.

"We don't have to get each other's names, but maybe a symbol," he replied. She was relieved he had said that without her having to make sure. It was clear that he wanted it to be a symbol of their relationship, but he wasn't being stupid about it either, and she could appreciate that.

Surprisingly, Mia did like the idea even though it was scary. It could be the perfect time to get her Omen tattoo covered up as well as connect with Sage on a deeper level. She could kill two birds with one stone, and it seemed like a good time to do it. There was no reason for her to be scared of her future with Sage anymore. He had proved to her for a while that he didn't intend on going anywhere that didn't involve her being there with him.

"Okay, let's do it," she replied. She already had an idea in her head, something that would show Sage just how much he meant to her. She had been painting Sage for so long, and that had been her own secret way of expressing her feelings. She didn't mind getting something that he could see. After all, it was his idea, and that meant something. He was opening up to her in a way she hadn't expected.

"Are you sure?" he asked, obviously shocked that she had agreed when she had sounded against it.

"Yes, I want to do this," she replied. She was sure that she would do anything for him. She wanted him to know that she was by his side through thick and thin. He was her life.

Mia watched as Sage grinned at her response. She could tell he was happy that she would take the step with him. They headed out to a tattoo shop after having a quick shower and breakfast.

"We don't want to pass out now, do we?" Sage joked as they ate. He made light of the matter, clearly completely committed to the idea. Mia could see it all over his face. It felt pretty amazing to have him be so sure of what he wanted all of a sudden. She didn't know if he would ever truly express himself with words, but Mia knew that actions spoke louder than words. She had never taken Sage for someone who would get a tattoo, and that surprised her the most. He didn't have a single tattoo on his body. She felt that it meant more that way. He was getting something out of his comfort zone, and that was something she could appreciate.

Mia could remember the first and only tattoo she had gotten when she joined the Omens. She remembered how the pain felt almost unbearable, and she had almost passed out because of it. She believed that it was because she knew she was making a mistake at the time and she thought that this time around she'd be fine. She wasn't doing this to prove that she could be trusted in a gang of horrible people, but she was doing it for Sage.

Within no time they were at a parlor as there was no point in prolonging the event. She felt nervous as they arrived outside the shop. She could hear the sound of the tattoo machines before they pushed the doors open. She had never really been into tattoos before. She had only gotten the Omens tattoo because she had wanted them to accept her and she knew that getting their symbol would be the only way. She had thought about covering it up for the longest time but had never gotten the courage until now. Even though it was scary she felt a sense of peace with the idea. She would do anything for Sage even if it meant getting something of him tattooed onto her skin.

"Hey there, how can I help you?" a tiny woman asked from behind the front counter.

"Hey, we're here to get some ink," Sage replied. "Is there anyone available who could help us?"

"That's rad. We have two artists available so you guys can get inked at the same time," she said. Within a few minutes, Sage and Mia went into separate booths so they could get tattooed. Neither of them knew what the other would get. It seemed to be an unspoken surprise between the two of them.

Mia had decided on a sprig of sage with a few flowers blooming from the top. She knew the sage would clearly show she belonged to Sage and that flowers indicated that their relationship was blooming. She knew that their relationship was stronger than it had ever been. She found it crazy how things could change so quickly. After all, it hadn't been that long ago that Sage had been completely different toward her. She could remember when he had been distant and almost horrible toward her, but all that had changed, and it definitely showed.

She loved her design. It had an embroidered effect to it that made it unique and special. Sage was special to her. He had been the whole time, and so she wanted to showcase that within her design. She sat in silence as she got tattooed. She tried to distract herself from the pain by humming to herself.

"You're not a fan of pain, are you?" the tattoo artist asked.

"Is it that obvious?" Mia replied with a small laugh.

"Haha, it's alright. Not everyone likes the pain, although there are a few freaks out there who do," the artist said. Mia couldn't imagine anyone enjoying the pain. It was almost unbearable.

"How can anyone like this pain? It's so bad," she replied.

"Well, your handling it pretty well I must admit, and luckily we're almost done."

Mia was relieved to hear that the tattoo was almost done. She wasn't sure how much longer she could take.

"Oh, thank goodness," she said. She had never been a fan of pain. Even growing up she had tried to make sure she didn't get injured. It may have had something to do with the fact that she couldn't stand the sight of blood, but she held herself together as the artist continued to shade in the leaves and added the detail that was necessary to give the effect she wanted. She knew Sage would have been going through similar pain, which made it easier for her to handle. She stayed focused on Sage and the step they were taking together that meant more than the pain. She closed her eyes and pictured him smiling at her, looking at her tattoo and loving it just as much as she did.

After another 30 minutes, the tattoo artist cleaned the tattoo and the surrounding area, making sure any ink that had been smudged around was cleaned off. Mia looked in the mirror at the artwork and was left speechless. As an artist herself, she was very particular about how she wanted things, and because it was going to be on her body for the rest of her life she wanted it to be perfect, and it was just that.

"It's even better than I had pictured, thank you so much," she said.

The best part of it all was the fact that she would never have to see the sign of the Omens on her skin for the rest of her life. That had definitely been one of the biggest mistakes she had made, and she could be happy to look at her body again and love what she saw because it had been too long since she had last been happy with her naked body.

The artist told her the instructions on how to clean

the tattoo and then told Mia she could leave. She left the booth and found Sage standing by the front desk, waiting for her. He was a sight for sore eyes. Mia just wanted to kiss him right then and there. She doubted he knew how crazy he drove her. If he moved and revealed just a bit of skin it would push her over the edge. Even them sharing the same bed and not being intimate had started to drive her crazy. She wondered if she had the same effect on him. He hadn't tried to make a move on her for a while.

## 18

Sage was over the moon when she agreed to get a tattoo. He knew it had been a big thing to suggest and also a big thing to do considering how painful it would be, but he thought it would be something they could share together, something that was theirs and that no one could take away. He had never done anything so extreme with anyone before, and he was happy that it was with Mia. She made him want to experience life more than he had before. He wanted to explore with her and possibly travel the world with her one day. She brought out a side of him that had been hidden for so long, he wanted to embrace it and hold on to it with both hands.

Maybe one day soon he'd be able to talk about the future. He wasn't 100 percent sure but there was definitely hope for him even after he had given up on thinking he would share his life with anyone. He knew Mia was good for him. She had helped him in so many ways that she didn't even know about. He hoped she knew on some level how much of an impact she had made on his life.

He had been a lonely ex-military man who had no love for life, no meaning that was truly getting him through but she had entered his life like a ray of sunshine, a rainbow that shone through all of his cloudy days. She was just what he needed. He was completely committed to her.

Sage knew he didn't have to prove anything to anyone, but he wanted to prove to Mia that he was committed to her. Maybe getting a tattoo together would seem childish to other people but he didn't care. No one else mattered more to him than Mia. It was crazy for him to think that he had tried so hard to push her away in the beginning. He had been such an idiot at the time, and he had almost lost her for good. He didn't want to think about how he had almost pushed her away.

"So what can I do for you today?" the tattoo artist assigned to him asked. She was a tattooed woman, covered almost head to toe with tattoos and also a lot of piercings. Sage had always found people with a huge amount of tattoos to be rather fascinating. Getting covered in tattoos wasn't exactly socially acceptable so it could ruin any potential for any other job opportunities. She was clearly dedicated to being a tattoo artist though. He admired her artwork, captivated by the story the woman had put on her body. Although he hadn't been a huge fan of tattoos, he could appreciate the work that went into them. Maybe it was also because he spent so much time with Mia that he had started to appreciate art more.

He pulled out a piece of paper with his tattoo design and showed it to the artist. He had managed to look up a design that he really loved while Mia had been getting ready. When he saw it, he knew immediately that it was what he wanted.

"I'd like something like this, but instead of the flowers around it I'd like it to have a piece of sage in its mouth," he replied. He had thought long and hard about his design before he had asked Mia if she would be okay with getting a tattoo. If he had been willing to share his idea with her he probably would have asked her to design it herself, but he wanted it to be a surprise. It would be a surprise for everyone.

"Okay, that's cool. Would you like to keep it that simple?" the tattoo artist asked.

"Yes, please. I'd like it to be soft just like the picture," he replied.

He knew the deeper meaning behind the tattoo, and he wanted it to be simple and almost elegant. After all, he wasn't a gangster of any kind, so he didn't need anything to represent how tough he was.

After the tattoo artist set everything up, the process started instantly. They didn't talk much during the time because Sage closed his eyes and focused on his breathing. He hadn't expected the pain to be as much as it was so he had to focus on keeping still instead of slapping the artist away. After a few hours of pain, Sage could finally look at his tattoo. He loved it, and he hoped Mia would love it too. He had learned over some time that Mia was strong and capable of pretty much anything and to him, he wanted to show her that he recognized that.

He had decided to get the tattoo on the back of his hand. That way, everyone would always be able to see it, they all had to know that he belonged to Mia. It wasn't that he was her property, but he knew that if anyone saw his tattoo, they would immediately know what it meant. The tattoo artist had done an amazing job, and Sage stared at the tattoo for some time before he could say thank you. He was left a little speechless.

"It's amazing, thank you so much," he said.

"I'm glad you're happy with it. Now for the healing process, I'd like you to clean it twice a day, once in the morning and once in the evening for only a week. You should look at some of our products in the front. We have a few balms that you can use to make sure it peels nicely, that's important. You can't leave it to dry out too much," she said with a warning look.

"Got it," he replied. He knew he'd do what he had to do to make sure the tattoo healed properly. He hadn't gone through a few hours of pain for it to amount to nothing.

He was extremely pleased with the tattoo, and he was so proud of himself for coming up with the idea on his own. He hoped Mia would love it just as much as he did. He was also interested to see what she had gotten done since they hadn't shown each other their designs.

He really wanted to show her as soon as he was out of the booth, but she was still busy with hers, so he had to wait and he decided to settle the bill while he waited.

## 19

After a few hours, Mia left her booth and joined Sage. They were both excited to show each other their tattoos.

"Wow," they both breathed at the same time as they exposed their tattoos.

"Your tattoo is stunning," Mia said as she looked at it closely. It was a lioness with sage in its mouth; it was breathtaking. It was soft and elegant, but the look in its eyes held a lot of power and strength.

"The lioness is you. I'm all yours," Sage said. He wanted to make sure Mia understood the true meaning behind his tattoo. Mia smiled at him. She wanted to smother his face with kisses in return. She was taken aback by the gesture he had made. It meant more to her than she could ever put into words.

Mia hadn't expected Sage to get something so meaningful, something so direct. She knew that when he suggested tattoos, it would mean something and although they hadn't told each other what they would get, Mia was shocked that Sage had made it so obvious to everyone that he was with Mia. It was only through the tattoo that he was showing Mia herself that he was with her. The lioness was probably one of the most beautiful references to Mia she had ever gotten. She knew she was strong but not many people had complimented her on it before, and so it was nice to see that out of all her qualities Sage appreciated the fact that she was strong.

They took each other's hand and left the tattoo parlor completely giddy. They were both over the moon with the outcome of their tattoos. It was a moment that they could share together and cherish, something that both of them could hold on to forever. Mia wanted to paint her tattoo, make a physical copy of it so whenever she wanted to, she could look at it in all its glory.

They made their way home.

"I think we both deserve a relaxed night in," Sage said as he opened the front door. Their home felt even more like their home now that they were on a completely different level of love and happiness. It seemed surreal that they had only started opening up to each other a few days before.

"I definitely agree, that was a painful process. Worth

it but painful," Mia replied. There was no way she could see herself standing in the kitchen cooking any sort of meal for them, and she was glad Sage had the same idea she did.

"I don't think either of us should cook tonight. Let's order in and watch movies tonight. We've earned it," he said.

"That's a great idea!" she replied. All she wanted to do was be with Sage in any way she could, and the idea of vegging out for the remainder of the day seemed like the cherry on top of an already wonderful day.

Neither of them said out loud what the tattoos meant, but when Sage told Mia he was committed to her and that he was hers, she felt extremely happy. She could think about their future and be sure that he would stick around after all. She was completely head over heels for him, and she knew that she would give her life for him if she had to. She had never seen herself as that type of person before, but she had also never felt that way for anyone before. It was almost a shock to her system as she realized how much he meant to her.

For the rest of the day, Mia and Sage snuggled up and watched movies together, enjoying each other's company. They got snacks and surrounded themselves with junk food and juice while they laughed and joked around with each other. They were both on cloud nine while they shared each other's company again. It felt even better than all the other times they had been together because they were both so giddy after getting their tattoos.

"This has honestly been one of the best days of my life," Mia said halfway through a movie as she looked over at Sage, eyeing his tattoo again. The look of it still shocked her. It was one of the greatest things anyone had ever done for her, and she was completely smitten with Sage for doing it.

"I know what you mean, it's been so amazing. It's all because of you, you know that, right?" Sage asked as he placed his hand on the side of her face, gently rubbing her cheek. She sighed at his touch, it was almost heavenly.

"It was your idea so technically it's because of you," Mia said shyly as she looked into his eyes.

"But if it weren't for you I wouldn't have needed to do it," he stated as he leaned forward and kissed her on the cheek. Mia moved her head and placed her lips on Sage's. She hadn't kissed him in so long, and after getting tattoos together, she just wanted to be as close to him as she possibly could. She wrapped her arms around his neck, bringing him closer to her while he wrapped his arms around her waist.

They were sitting on the couch, so they had to twist their bodies to face each other. The kiss was filled with passion and lust, also love. They had made a huge commitment to each other, and with the feeling of happiness hanging in the air, they just wanted to be together.

Mia worked her way onto Sage's lap, straddling him as she took his face between her hands so she could kiss him deeply. Meanwhile, Sage wrapped his arms around her waist and slid his one hand up to the small of her back. They wanted each other.

"I've forgotten how your lips feel against mine," Mia said as she kissed his cheeks, leaving a trail behind as she moved down his neck.

"I've been wanting to kiss you so bad lately, but I've been waiting for the right time," he replied as he moved his hands to her face so he could move her head to look into her eyes.

"This is the perfect moment," she said as she leaned forward to kiss him once more. Their need for each other grew as the kiss got hot and heavy. Their hands roamed over each other's bodies as the kiss grew deeper. Their mouths opened so their tongues could brush against each other, both of them needing to taste the other.

"Let's go to bed," Sage suggested. Mia could already feel a stiffness beneath her. She liked the idea of going to bed with him and not just to sleep. She shifted off of him and took his hand, leading him to his room. He followed close behind her, watching hungrily as her hips swayed in front of him, his desire for her growing while the bulge in his pants grew harder.

Mia pulled him into her after she closed the door behind her, needing her lips to be against his again. She tugged at his shirt, grabbing the bottom of it so she could pull it over his head. He allowed her to take control of the moment as he lifted his arms above his head. Sage didn't waste time and did the same to Mia, removing her shirt, so she stood with just her bra and pants on.

"You're so sexy," he said as he kissed her, moving down her neck and toward her chest, bringing his hands behind her so he could unclasp her bra. He wanted and needed Mia. It was not just a desperate need for her but a need that was filled with love and happiness.

Sage had had sex for the sake of it before. He had also just fucked women because there wasn't a lot of emotion behind it, but it was different with Mia. Every time they had been intimate it had meant something, and it meant more now than ever before. They made their way to his bed, never letting go of each other as they moved, their bodies in a state of constant connection. That night they didn't fuck as they had before, that night they made love like neither of them had before.

They were wrapped up in each other, allowing all their emotions to come across through the way they held each other, through the way they touched each other. It was all desire and love. It felt different and new to both of them. Neither of them had experienced a connection so strong with another person. If they could have, they would've stayed forever in the bubble they had created for themselves. It was almost overwhelming to think of the feelings they both had for each other.

They made love that night and the words 'I love you' hung in the air between them. Neither of them said it, but it was obvious that they both felt it. Mia knew she wouldn't say it until he did, but she could feel it when he touched her. It wasn't just the desire of being naked anymore, and it wasn't just the physical attraction between them that drew them together. It had grown into something so much more than that.

They fell asleep content and fulfilled.

*Sage looked around him and saw the inside of his house, the house he had with Mia. It was different from what he was used to seeing. It had pictures on the walls, paintings of sunsets and hearts. He walked up to the paintings, looking at all of them in turn, and took in all the details.*

*They were beautifully painted, and each brushstroke connected perfectly with the next. He walked over to the picture of the sunset, and in his head, he knew exactly where the inspiration had come from.*

*"That was one of the best days we've had together," Mia said as she stood next to him, taking his hand in hers as she admired the painting with him.*

*"You are so talented, Mia. I mean this is amazing," he replied as he continued to stare at the painting before him.*

*She had captured the light and colors so well, the different shades of pink, orange, and yellow reflecting off of the ocean were immaculate. He turned around the room so he could look at the rest of the paintings, all of them as breathtakingly detailed and stunning as the last.*

*"Thank you, but also thank you for giving me the memories and the reason to paint these," she said with a gentle squeeze of his hand.*

*He stood there with Mia at his side, captivated by the person she was. She was the definition of perfect to him and a dream come true.*

Sage no longer had dreams of Laura, and he also no longer had bad dreams. His mind and heart were focused on Mia which he was happy about. He didn't have to worry about falling asleep anymore, and he didn't have to worry about screaming himself awake. He knew he'd still have to work on a lot of the damage and pain he carried with him, but the improvement was more than he could have ever asked for. Mia didn't know that her body next to his helped him and it was a secret he would keep to himself. He worried that because she was a creative person her mind would probably dramatize his dreams to be more than they were. He didn't want to give her any nightmares.

Sage and Mia both smiled in their sleep, both were

dreaming of their lives together. They were on a new path together, and they couldn't wait to see what the future would hold for them.

It seemed that their relationship had finally reached a level where they were both completely happy and blissful. The future could hold so much for them after the step they had taken to create a stronger and more unbreakable bond. Neither of them really felt any sort of need to worry about what they could handle going forward. They had gone through so much already so anything that came their way, they could get through.

## 20

Mia woke up with her body intertwined with Sage; it was pure bliss. She had never thought that she would get a tattoo with him, and after everything, she thought they would've kept their distance after he came back from the hospital. She had never expected him to change his mind when it came to her. He had seemed so sure of his decision to keep his distance from her, and so being with him was a surprise. She didn't mind it, of course. She had wanted it all along, and she smiled to herself as she looked over to Sage who was still fast asleep. She didn't want to get up, and she didn't want to leave him just yet. There was nothing urgent for her to attend to so she decided to stay in bed with him.

She wrapped herself around him, and in his sleep, Sage nuzzled closer to her, inhaling as he laid his head in the crook of her neck while he spooned her from behind. Mia's heart soared with happiness as she closed her eyes and drifted back to sleep.

*Mia was in a good mood as she walked around the grocery store. She pushed a trolley in front of her that was filled with food items. She leaned into the trolley and pulled out a bar of chocolate that lay hidden beneath a box of cereal. She craved the chocolate so badly she couldn't wait any longer as she rooted the packaging open and bit into the milky chocolate content.*

*"Hmm," she said. She was, of course, going to pay for it when they checked out.*

*"Sharing is caring, you know," Sage said from beside her. She eyed him as he watched her take another bite.*

*"You know how I feel about sharing chocolate," she said as she swallowed but as much as she wanted to prove her point, she decided to share her chocolate with him. They shared everything, so there was no point in keeping chocolate away from him.*

*With a slight laugh, Sage took a bite of the chocolate. He didn't have much of a sweet tooth, so one bite was good enough for him.*

*"We should probably leave before you either eat all the chocolate they have on their shelves or before you buy all their food," he said mockingly as he looked into the trolley. It was almost filled to the top.*

*"You should know better than to bring a hungry woman to*

*the shops, especially when she's eating for two," she said as she rubbed the tiny bump that was protruding from her stomach.*

*"You can't use the baby as an excuse," Sage laughed as he too placed his hand on her belly.*

*"Yes, I can because I'm right," she huffed as she ate the last bite of her chocolate. She knew she technically couldn't use the baby as an excuse but she would anyway. Not even Sage could fight with her logic, and he wouldn't fight with her either way.*

*They were still newly married, but the excitement of a baby had made their bond stronger. Neither of them wished things were different even though it hadn't been planned.*

In her sleep, Mia sighed with happiness. She knew that getting married and having children might never be something in the future with Sage. He had tried to avoid any conversations that involved too much of the future, but Mia would be lying if she said she didn't picture herself having a few children with him. It would be the best thing she could ever imagine happening to her with regard to him.

A few more blissful hours of sleep passed them by, and soon they were both up to tackle the day. They both showered and cleaned their tattoos which hurt just a bit but both of them had lived through worse, so it didn't bother them too much.

"How is your tattoo?" Sage asked as they were both in the kitchen having coffee. Her hip stung a bit after cleaning it.

"It was fine before I cleaned it, but it's not too bad. And yours?" she asked in return. She stared at his beautiful piece of artwork and she still couldn't believe it was for her.

"It's just fine," he replied with a gentle smile.

"No regrets?" she asked. Although it had been his idea, she was still worried he'd come to regret it. It was a rather spur of the moment decision after all.

"None whatsoever," he said.

She was glad she didn't regret it either. The fact that they both had chosen something to symbolize each other was pretty amazing too. Their ideas had been so alike.

They spent some of the day together, talking over breakfast before Sage went to his office to do some work while Mia did some painting.

Mia received a call from the Hell Kats in the early afternoon. They needed her to go back to the bar because Lorraine had shown up again. She was going to chat to her the day after she had taken her home the last time, but things got in the way, and with a sore hip from her recent tattoo Mia had also pushed it to the side thinking it wouldn't be necessary yet, kind of hoping Lorraine would have gotten the picture already.

It was clear she hadn't, or she just didn't care. Either way, it annoyed Mia that she was still around after the scene she had caused the last time. She really wasn't someone they wanted around. Her presence hadn't brought anything good to anyone, and she seemed to drink too much.

When she arrived at the club, she could see that Lorraine was drunk again, and this time it wasn't even 1 pm. Either she was an alcoholic or had some serious issues she needed to work on. Mia could never understand what could drive a person to be so intoxicated so early in the day. Whatever the reason was, Lorraine needed help in the long run. If she drank as regularly as it seemed then there was definitely something wrong with her.

Mia had never been one for drinking. Sure she had gotten into drugs, but that had been completely different. She had always felt drinking was just a waste of time. Many people would disagree, of course. You were more likely to die from an overdose than a few drinks when you think about it, but drinking had never done it for Mia. Maybe it was because she always wanted more, wanted more of a high, more of a feeling. She wasn't sure but drinking just didn't seem like a good idea, especially when out in public and you had no control over what could be said to those around you.

"Lorraine, why are you here again?" she asked as she stared at her. Lorraine looked at Mia and instantly got mad.

"It's because of you that I had to get a taxi here so I

could get my car!" Lorraine yelled as she picked up her hand, made a fist and tried to hit Mia. However, because she was drunk, she missed completely, and her body swayed as she tried to keep her balance. It was shocking that she had tried to hit her. Everyone in the club settled to watch what would happen next. They all knew Mia shouldn't be messed with, and anyone was stupid to even try.

"You were in no state to drive, and clearly you've had too much to drink again," Mia replied with narrowed eyes. She couldn't believe Lorraine was mad at her for making sure she got home safely. After all, it really wasn't her job to look after drunk people.

Out of nowhere, Lorraine settled her head in her hands and started to cry. She was so overwhelmed with emotions that her cries sounded pained. Mia couldn't understand how someone could go from one extreme to the other. It was clear she was mentally unstable. Whatever had caused her to drink so much was clearly making her go a little crazy. Her mood swings were all over the place, and she had hardly made any sense all three times Mia had been around her.

"Sage used to love me," she cried. It took Mia a few seconds to realize what she had said. The shock of it drowned out all the other noises in the club, although most of the noise had stopped already.

"What?" she asked. She had no other words as her

mind went into overdrive, thinking of what this woman could possibly mean. If she knew Sage, why hadn't she tried to greet him the first time he had been with Mia? It was confusing.

"You heard me. He's not supposed to love you, he's supposed to love me. We were going to get married and live happily ever after before everything changed. Before I changed," she sobbed. Mia couldn't understand what she meant by what she had said. How had she changed? She thought that if Sage had not recognized her, it must have been because she had changed her face.

Why would she have changed her face though, Mia thought. Not many people just changed their faces, and their entire faces at that so Mia found it really strange. It didn't make sense at all in her mind. Also, if Sage had loved this woman why would she have changed her face in the first place. It seemed to be a bit of an extreme act for someone to go through.

Mia herself had never thought about reconstructive surgery. She had luckily always been happy with her body besides the minor weight changes she went through which she could easily fix herself by going to the gym. It had always been a simple fix. She would never understand why women would do something so drastic to themselves. She could understand only if that person didn't completely love the self which was rather common in society, but Mia turned to focus on Lorraine as her mind had started to wonder. She looked closely at her face and couldn't see any scarring from any form of surgery. It would be a strange thing to lie about, though.

Had her drinking driven Sage away, had she gotten worse because he left her? There were so many questions going around in Mia's mind. None of them she said out loud though. She was too confused to make complete sentences. She didn't know what to ask Lorraine or if she should even bother asking in the first place. She was extremely intoxicated and saying a lot of random things while Mia thought quietly to herself. She could be on some sort of drug for all Mia knew, although she had a lot of experience with drugs and her behavior didn't match anything Mia knew.

None of it made any sense to her, and the more she thought about it, the more her head hurt. There were just too many questions and warning signals going off in her head. She knew the only way she could get the answers she needed was to ask Sage or wait until Lorraine was sober but with the amount of alcohol she had consumed, Mia would have to wait quite a while, and she didn't have the patience for that sort of thing.

"I don't understand. Are you saying you and Sage were together once?" Mia asked after a while, completely confused by the situation. Sage had never told her about his past relationships, so she wasn't sure if Lorraine was telling the truth or not. But she was a crazy woman. She had shown that the day she had first tried to break into the office. She didn't have much of a good reputation but why would she lie, what would she have to gain?

"Duh, you're not very bright, are you?" Lorraine said as she wiped tears off of her cheeks. She didn't seem to notice that she had formed a bit of an attitude or rather she just didn't have a filter anymore to contain what she said and how she said it. Mia wanted to slap her. She was confusing her and insulting her all in one go, and that didn't make matters any better. She knew that wouldn't be a good idea though so with an itching hand, Mia continued to stare at Lorraine, unsure of what to say or do next.

Lorraine hadn't presented herself well from the get-go, and Mia knew that after all, she had seemed stupid from their first meeting. If anything Mia wanted to call her stupid but decided against it so she held her tongue so the words wouldn't slip out.

Mia couldn't believe what she was hearing, but she wasn't sure if she was lying or not. Sage hadn't opened up to her about his past yet. He hadn't told her much at all so she couldn't be sure what his relationships in the past were like. She wasn't naive enough to assume he had been single all of his life because he was a very attractive man, but Sage had seen Lorraine before, and he hadn't said anything. Was he trying to keep it a secret? It didn't make any sense. Nothing made sense to Mia.

For the first time in a long time, Mia wanted a drink. Better yet she wouldn't have minded something to numb her feelings completely. She couldn't think straight the longer she sat there, trying to think through everything at a logical level. There was no logic behind it though. Nothing was making sense to Mia, and it was driving her crazy.

"I'm his true love, and he'll come back to me," Lorraine continued, her words slightly slurred because of how drunk she was. Her gibberish got worse as time went on.

"Sage doesn't know you though," Mia said. At least he acted as if he didn't know her when he had seen her a few days ago.

"Of course, he wouldn't recognize me. I have a different face and a different name. He will know soon enough though. Back then my name was Laura. I've come back for him," she said matter of factly. Mia was confused even more by what she had said. What did she mean that she had come back for him?

Mia didn't know what to say in return. She didn't know much about the woman, and when she thought about it she still didn't know too much about Sage, but she still trusted him, and she felt that he wouldn't lie about anything. She knew that his past was painful to talk about, and she had been extremely understanding toward him, so she hadn't pushed the topic much. She wanted him to open up to her in his own time because then she would know that he trusted her, but she had gotten a tattoo with him to show him what he meant to her. Could there be things he was still keeping from her? She couldn't understand why nor did she believe that Sage could be seeing another woman behind her back. They lived and breathed around each other day in and day out. There wasn't much time for him to hide that sort of thing from her.

Could this woman just be crazy, or was she telling the truth? Mia couldn't be sure.

Could she really be someone from Sage's past that he had tried to hide, or was she just a past lover that didn't want to let go? Mia had a lot of questions, and Sage would be the only one with all the answers.

She knew she had to get back to him as soon as she could, Lorraine was making her brain hurt with all the uncertainty, but she also didn't want to take her word before hearing Sage's side of the story. Maybe he could clear it all up for her, reassure her that Lorraine was just crazy and she was just trying to ruin what they had out of jealousy, but even as she thought about it they hadn't been together in front of her so she couldn't have seen much to be jealous of.

A part of Mia was certain that getting the tattoos so

soon without really talking would be bad luck, and she had been proven right. Everything changed within less than 24 hours, and she wasn't sure how things would be going forward. Sage had a lot of explaining to do, and she would try to hear him out first before she lost her mind.

She left the club and phoned Sage outside, leaving Lorraine exactly where she was, she didn't care about her. She needed to hear what Sage had to say immediately.

**DARK DESIRES**
~ A billionaire dark romance series ~
Dark Desire
Dark Rules
Dark Secret
Dark Time
Dark Truth

**BARRE TO BAR**
~ A billionaire second chance series ~
Dancing With Lies
Dancing With Temptation
Dancing With Doubt
Dancing With Guilt
Dancing With Redemption

# TWISTED INTENTION
~ A billionaire revenge romance series ~
Twisted Beauty
Twisted Love
Twisted Fate

## Mafia's Obsession
~ A hot mafia romance series ~
Mafia's Dirty Secret
Mafia's Fake Bride
Mafia's Final Play

## Screaming Demons
~ An MC romance series full of suspense ~
Rough Start
Rough Ride
Rough Choice
Rough Patch
Rough Return
Rough Road
Rough Trip
Rough Night
Rough Love

## Standalone Contemporary Romance
Billionaire in Vegas
Billionaire Hunt

Billionaire's Game
Billionaire Retreat
Billionaire On Air
A Chance To Love
Somebody To Love
Not Mine To Love


Check out Summer's entire collection at
**www.summercooper.com/books**

# ABOUT SUMMER COOPER

Thank you so much for reading. Without you, it wouldn't be possible for me to be a full-time author. I hope you enjoy reading my books as much as I do writing them.

Besides (obviously!) reading and writing, I also love cuddling my dogs, shouting at Alexa, being upside down (aka Yoga) and driving my family cray-cray!

Get in touch at
hello@summercooper.com
www.summercooper.com

facebook.com/summercooperauthor
instagram.com/summercooperauthor
goodreads.com/summercooper
bookbub.com/profile/summer-cooper